THE GREEK
BOSS'S BRIDE

THE GREEK BOSS'S BRIDE

BY

CHANTELLE SHAW

First published in Great Britain 2006
Large Print edition 2007
Harlequin Mills & Boon Limited,
Eton House, 18-24 Paradise Road,
Richmond, Surrey TW9 1SR

© Chantelle Shaw 2006

ISBN-13: 978 0 263 19450 0
ISBN-10:   0 263 19450 7

Set in Times Roman 16½ on 19¼ pt.
16-0507-55186

Printed and bound in Great Britain
by Antony Rowe Ltd, Chippenham, Wiltshire

PROLOGUE

NIKOS NIARCHOU'S VISIT to the London offices of the Niarchou Leisure Group was the subject of intense excitement among all the staff. All the staff bar one, Kezia thought impatiently, as she crossed the reception area and was assailed by the overpowering smell of furniture polish.

'Anyone would think we were expecting a visit from royalty,' she muttered to Jo Stafford, her colleague from the PR department, as they stepped into the lift.

'A visit from the company chairman is as good as,' Jo replied seriously. 'It's over a year since he last came, and the MD is sweating buckets that we make a good impression. Nik Niarchou demands high standards from every member of staff, from top management down to office junior. You *must* remember him,' she added, when Kezia failed to look suitably overawed.

'I joined the company just after his last visit. I remember there was a lot of talk about it, but I've never met him so I'm afraid I don't know what all the fuss is about.'

'You must have heard about him, though,' Jo protested. 'His reputation in the bedroom is almost as legendary as it is in the boardroom. The gossip columns can't get enough of him— but let's face it: he's a gorgeous Greek multi-millionaire who has the added attraction of being single. It's not surprising he grabs the head-lines—especially now he's decided to settle per-manently in England. Apparently he's bought some fantastic stately home in Hertfordshire called Otterbourne House, and there's a queue a mile long for the position of lady of the manor.'

The lift stopped at Kezia's floor and she stepped out. 'You'd better point this demi-god out to me when he arrives. It could prove embar-rassing if I don't recognise him,' she added dryly.

'You'll know him,' Jo assured her with a grin. 'Nik Niarchou is unlike any man you've ever met. Trust me, he's unforgettable.'

Kezia hurried past the front desk of the PR department and shook her head at the sight of the receptionist, who was measuring the length of each tulip stalk before placing the bloom carefully in a vase.

The whole place had gone mad, she thought irritably, and all because of one man. How great could he be? Jo had described Nikos Niarchou as some sort of Greek colossus, but it was amazing how blinding the lure of money could be. In reality he was probably short, balding and middle aged—with a paunch, Kezia added for good measure. However, there was no denying the fact that as company chairman, Mr Niarchou was supremely powerful. It was reputed that he had impossibly high standards and she prayed that her boss, Frank Warner, would actually make it into the office on time and sober this morning.

By ten-thirty Frank hadn't shown up, and she was panicking. She had worked as PA to the head of the Niarchou Group's public relations department for the past year, and had to admit that the job was not quite as she had anticipated. Her boss was struggling to cope with an acrimonious divorce and a drink problem. She wasn't sure which one had triggered the other, but she couldn't go on covering for him for much longer without other members of staff noticing. She was fond of Frank, but right now she could cheerfully boil him in oil, Kezia thought darkly as she walked along to the coffee machine and stared down at the car park, searching for his car.

There was no sign of him, and with a groan she headed back along the corridor.

'Damn it, Frank, where are you?' she muttered, halting abruptly in the doorway of her office as a figure swung round from the window.

Her first impression of the man who turned towards her was his exceptional height. He was easily five inches over six feet tall, she estimated, unable to drag her gaze from the formidable width of his shoulders. His black, impeccably tailored suit sheathed a lean, hard body, and she noted the impressive muscle definition of his abdomen visible beneath his silk shirt. As if in slow motion she lifted her eyes to his face—and swallowed as the full impact of his handsome face overwhelmed her. Razor-sharp cheekbones, a square jaw that hinted an implacably determined character, and a mouth that was wide, full-lipped and innately sensual.

Jo had been right, Kezia acceded numbly. Nikos Niarchou was unlike any man she had ever met.

There was no doubt in her mind that the man who was watching her with the silent stillness of a predator *was* the head of the phenomenally successful Niarchou Group. He possessed an air of authority teamed with a barely concealed impatience. But nothing had prepared her for his raw sexual magnetism—or her reaction to it.

'That's a very good question, Miss Trevellyn. Where exactly *is* Frank Warner?'

His voice was deep timbred, with a pronounced Greek accent that was so sexy it made her toes curl. *Get a grip,* she told herself fiercely, irritated by the discovery that she seemed to have lost the power of speech.

His dark eyes travelled over her in a slow appraisal, noting the simplicity of her grey skirt and white blouse, and Kezia crossed her arms instinctively over her chest, longing for the protection of her jacket. Her clothes were smart and practical, but beneath his intense scrutiny she was aware that her blouse gaped fraction-

ally over her breasts and her skirt clung faith-
fully to her curvaceous hips and rounded
bottom. His gaze moved lower and skimmed
her legs in their sheer black hose before
trawling up again, and she had the feeling that
he had mentally stripped her bare, leaving her
exposed to his gaze.

With a huge effort she forced herself to relax
and moved further into the room. 'You have the
advantage of knowing my name, but I'm afraid
I don't know yours—Mr…?'

'Niarchou—Nikos Niarchou.'

The gleam in his eyes warned her that he was
amused by her pretence that she did not know his
identity. He dismantled her air of cool efficiency
with humiliating ease, and she blushed as she prof-
fered her hand to formalise their introduction.

'And you are Kezia Trevellyn, Frank's personal
assistant.'

His hand closed around hers and instantly
engulfed it. She had expected the contact to be
brief and impersonal, but incredibly he lifted her
hand to his mouth and pressed his lips against her
fingers. It was electrifying; she almost literally
felt sparks shoot down her arm. Her whole body

was on fire, and with a gasp she tore her fingers free from his grasp.

Her legs felt distinctly wobbly as a mixture of embarrassment and fierce sexual heat coursed through her veins. She had never felt anything remotely like it before. It was like being hit by a bulldozer. Jo hadn't lied when she'd said Nik Niarchou was unforgettable. Kezia knew instinctively that his darkly handsome features would be imprinted on her brain for ever. But from somewhere she salvaged a little of her self-possession and glanced at him coolly.

'Yes, I'm Frank Warner's PA, but I'm afraid he's out of the office this morning.' She crossed to her desk and made a show of flicking through the diary. 'His meeting is scheduled to finish around lunchtime. If there's something you need to discuss with him, I'll ask him to call you as soon as he gets back.' She awarded him an impersonal smile and moved towards the door, her body language clearly indicating that she expected him to follow her.

Instead he pulled out the chair from behind the desk and sat down.

'Come and take a seat, Miss Trevellyn—or can I call you Kezia?'

The gleam in his eyes told her he would call her what he liked, with or without her permission. He was patently a man who liked his own way, and she was aware that for Frank's sake she had better curb her hot temper.

Once she was seated opposite him he subjected her to a long, hard stare until she shifted restlessly. His expression was unfathomable, his eyes shaded by long black lashes that matched the colour of his hair. This close she caught the subtle tang of his cologne, and her senses flared. She couldn't think straight, and try as she might she seemed to be physically unable to prevent her gaze from straying to his mouth.

'What's going on, Kezia?' he demanded abruptly, the harshness of his tone making her jump. 'We're both aware that Frank's diary is as empty this week as last. I glanced through it before you came in,' he added blandly, plainly unconcerned by her indignant gasp.

'You had no right to snoop through my desk—' she began, her voice faltering as his brows lifted fractionally. He was the company chairman, he had the right to do what he damn well liked and they both knew it.

'Where is he now? The pub?'

'At eleven o'clock in the morning! Of course not—' She broke off and tucked a stray copper-coloured curl behind her ear. 'It's true Frank has had some difficulties in his private life recently,' she admitted slowly. 'I understand that his divorce from his wife was very bitter.'

'And what part did *you* play in the ending of his marriage?' Nik's hard expression did not flicker as twin spots of colour flared on Kezia's cheeks.

'I'm sorry? Why should Frank's divorce have anything to do with me?'

'It's not unheard of for a man of a certain age to make a fool of himself over his much younger secretary. Especially when that secretary is an attractive woman like yourself,' he added coolly, ignoring the sparks of fury in her eyes. 'Your loyalty to your boss is admirable, Kezia, but I'm curious to understand why you would lie in defence of a man who I understand is out of the office more often that he's in it. Word is, you're carrying Frank. The success of the last ad campaign was solely down to you, although you allowed him to take the credit.'

'And my loyalty to him is proof that I'm

sleeping with him?' Kezia snapped, trembling with outrage. 'Frank's a friend and colleague, nothing more, and to imply otherwise is hideous.'

She jumped to her feet and glared at Nik Niarchou across the desk. Sinfully sexy and as arrogant as hell, she surmised darkly. He was also far more aware of the problems within the PR department than she had credited, and she feared there was little she could do to help Frank Warner.

'So, if it's not an affair it must be the drink,' Nik mused. 'You have to appreciate that the situation can't carry on, Kezia.' He rose to his feet, towering over her so that she was forced to crane her neck to look at him.

'What will you do? Frank's a good man…' she muttered as he strolled over to the door. She scurried after him. For a moment she thought he was going to ignore her, but then he turned and glanced down at her anxious face.

'Obviously there will need to be changes,' he told her bluntly.

To her consternation he caught hold of her chin and tilted her face so her eyes locked with his. Instantly her senses quivered. He was a sorcerer, and she was held powerless in his spell. He would be an incredible lover, she acknowledged numbly as liquid heat flooded through her veins. His eyes narrowed, his body suddenly taut, and she was mortified by the horrifying realisation that he must have read her mind.

'Your loyalty to Warner is misjudged but impressive, as is your work record. My PA has inconveniently decided to get married and move to Australia with her husband,' he informed her, and Kezia frowned at the unexpected change of subject. 'After ten years of dedicated service, Donna is deserting me.'

'With good reason, as far as I can see,' Kezia muttered, allowing her unruly tongue get the better of her. But to her surprise Nik flung his head back and laughed.

'Spirited as well as beautiful—a dangerous combination,' he drawled. 'But I like danger. It adds spice, don't you think, Kezia? The post of my PA will become available in the next couple of months. I'll look forward to receiving your application.'

'What makes you so sure I'd be interested?' she demanded crossly, irritated by his arrogance.

'Instinct,' he replied softly, his smile deepening as he noted the hectic colour on her cheeks. 'And I'm rarely wrong.'

CHAPTER ONE

NIK WAS DUE home any minute.

Kezia glanced at the clock on the dashboard and pressed her foot down on the accelerator. At this rate her dynamic and notoriously impatient boss would arrive at his country mansion ahead of her, and all hell would break loose. Nik was bringing a group of Bulgarian businessmen to Otterbourne House, hoping to impress them with his plans for a hotel complex on the Black Sea coast, and he expected his PA to be ready and waiting to greet his guests.

Could the day get any worse? Kezia wondered grimly as she peered through the rain. It was bad enough that the catering company she had booked for tonight's party had pulled out at the last minute. Most of the staff had come down with flu, the harassed administrator had explained. But with a day's notice to try and make alternative arrangements, Kezia had been short on sympathy. Fortunately Nik's housekeeper, Mrs Jessop, had rallied round, and was busy preparing a lavish dinner that was set to impress the guests. It had been left to Kezia to collect a selection of desserts from the patisserie, but the trip into town had taken longer than she had anticipated. The torrential downpour had caused serious flooding along the narrow country lanes, and now dusk was falling.

She needed to focus all her concentration on the road, but as usual it was a certain sexy Greek who dominated her thoughts. An unbidden image of Nik's handsome face filled her mind as she pictured his classically sculpted features. *Get a grip,* she admonished herself sternly, irritated at the way her heartbeat quickened with every mile that she drew nearer to Otterbourne.

He had been away for the past few weeks, visiting his family in Greece, and she was dismayed at how much she had missed him. It was pathetic for a grown woman of twenty-four to have developed such a ridiculous fixation with a man who was way out of her league, she reminded herself savagely. She felt like a teenager in the throes of her first crush and she would die of shame if he ever guessed how much he affected her.

She reached the outskirts of the village and breathed a sigh of relief. Another five minutes and she would be turning in to the gates leading to Otterbourne House. With any luck she would just beat Nik—although she would have little time to tidy her hair or check her make-up. Not that he would notice, she conceded bleakly. As far as Nik was concerned she was his ultra-efficient PA, whose sole purpose was to ensure that his life ran smoothly.

As he had explained at her interview, three months ago, he didn't want a decorative bimbo running his office; he was looking for someone who was prepared to put in long hours and who would blend unobtrusively into the background. With her unruly curls tamed into a sleek chignon, and her sensible navy blue suit, he had obviously deemed Kezia the ideal choice.

There had been no element of the sexual tension she recalled from their first meeting at the London head office—at least not on his part.

He'd given no indication that he even remembered her, and the fact that her tongue had tied itself in knots throughout the interview had added to her embarrassment. It was evident that he was only interested in her organisational skills, and sometimes she wondered whether he would notice if she paraded around the office stark naked.

Without warning something shot out from the shadows and ran in front of the car. Kezia hit the brakes, skidded on the wet road and lost control. She was heading for the trees, and with a frantic cry she jerked the wheel. The engine stalled and she ploughed into the bushes that lined the road. So much for concentrating, she thought shakily. The seat belt had saved her from serious injury, but the force of the impact had caused her to hit her head on the steering wheel, and already she could feel a lump the size of an egg swelling on her temple.

She restarted the engine and cautiously backed up onto the road before climbing out of the car. It was too dark to make a proper inspection for damage, but at least the car was drivable. A wave of sickness swept over her. What was it that had run out? Probably a fox that had now disappeared into the undergrowth, she told herself as she squinted through the rain. She was cold and wet, and running seriously late, but the thought of leaving an animal lying injured on the roadside was abhorrent to her, and with a muttered curse she began to search along the verge.

Ten minutes later she was soaked to the skin and ready to give up when a faint whimper drew her attention to the other side of the ditch. The dog was no more than a bag of bones. Its fur was wet and matted, and in the dark in was impossible to see if it was injured, but when she held out her hand it moved tentatively towards her.

'Come on, boy,' she whispered gently, feeling the animal tremble with a mixture of cold and fright as she lifted it into her arms. 'Let's get out of this rain.'

She waded back across the ditch, but as she scrabbled up the slippery bank she felt the heel of one of her shoes give way and cursed loudly. Her new kitten-heel shoes were ruined, and her skirt was covered in mud. Nik was going to go mad, Kezia acknowledged as she hobbled over to the car and deposited the dog on the front seat. He had spent the past week on the phone, relaying precise instructions for the weekend, and it was safe to assume that he would not be impressed when his PA turned up late, looking as if she'd been dragged through a hedge backwards.

Otterbourne House stood at the end of a long drive, hidden from view by tall conifers. Nikos Niarchou felt his heart lift as the limousine rounded the bend and he absorbed the classical elegance of his English country manor. It was good to be back, he thought with a surge of satisfaction—despite the rain. Much as he had enjoyed his trip to Greece, the past couple of weeks seemed to have lasted a lifetime.

It had been good to spend time with his family, but his parents' unsubtle hints about it being time for him to find a nice Greek girl and settle down had driven him mad. His mother had seized on his visit as an opportunity to nag him to slow his pace, assuring him that he looked tired and accusing him of overdoing things, but it had been the sight of his father, unexpectedly frail and looking every one of his eighty years, that had caused Nik to take a break from his hectic schedule.

Now he was eager to get back to work— starting with the presentation that he hoped would impress the Bulgarians into backing his plans for a hotel complex. He was confident that Kezia had organised tonight's reception with her usual efficiency. As he ushered his guests through the front door, he glanced around the entrance hall expectantly. Kezia was supposed to be here. He had specifically asked her to act as his hostess, and he frowned when his elderly housekeeper stepped forward to greet him.

'Where's Kezia?' he demanded, without preamble.

'Good evening, Mr Niarchou, it's good to have you back.'

'It's good to be back, Mrs Jessop.' His brief smile revealed a flash of white teeth that contrasted with his olive gold skin but failed to add warmth to his dark eyes. 'I was expecting Kezia to be here,' he muttered in an impatient undertone. 'Where the hell is she?'

He had spent a trying day entertaining the Bulgarian businessmen and their wives aboard his private jet, the language barrier having proved an exasperating obstacle to conversation.

He needed his PA here, damn it. Corporate entertaining was one of Kezia's duties, and he had planned to leave his guests in her capable hands while he took a break to shower and unwind. He had given specific orders, and he did not expect them to be flouted without a very good reason.

'There were some problems with the caterers. All sorted now,' the housekeeper hastily reassured him, 'but Kezia had to run into town. She'll be here any minute, I'm sure.'

'I hope so.'

Nik's frown deepened in annoyance. He had come to rely on his PA over the past three months. Sensible and efficient, Kezia was an ideal employee, who could be relied upon to get on with her work without fuss. Beneath her calm demeanour she possessed a sharp wit that made conversations with her interesting—as he had discovered the first time he had met her at the London office. He was a man who liked to have his own way, yet he was secretly amused by Kezia's refusal to let him dominate her. He had missed her while he was away, he realised with a flicker of surprise and he was looking forward to renewing their discussions on everything from politics to the arts.

His eyes narrowed as the drawing room door opened and a familiar figure emerged. 'What is Miss Harvey doing here?' he muttered under his breath to his housekeeper. Tania Harvey, his current mistress, was a sinful siren, with a body to die for, but she had little else to offer other than an encyclopaedic knowledge of celebrity gossip— and he was not in the mood to listen to hours of tittle-tattle about life on the modelling circuit.

'I understand she's joining you for dinner,' Mrs Jessop replied brightly.

'At whose invitation?' There was no disguising the irritation in Nik's voice and Mrs Jessop shrugged helplessly.

'I don't know. I assumed you… Perhaps Kezia invited her?' she murmured. 'That sounds like her car now—you can ask her.'

'I intend to. Believe me.'

Tania was walking towards him, and with a supreme effort Nik stifled his impatience as she wrapped her arms around his neck.

'Hello, darling. Welcome home,' she murmured, pouting prettily in the way he had once found a turn-on but which was now as annoying as her overtly proprietary air. He had no intention of allowing Tania or any other woman to consider Otterbourne as *home*—at least not for the foreseeable future.

'Tania, what a charming surprise—I hadn't realised you would be here,' he greeted her politely, as he disentangled himself from her grasp.

'Your PA invited me—I assumed on your behalf.' The pout deepened. 'You are pleased to see me, aren't you, Nik? Kezia was most insistent that I joined you for dinner.'

'Was she? That was very thoughtful of her,' he murmured dryly. 'Naturally I'm pleased to see you, but I'm afraid I'm going to be busy for most of the weekend.'

'Lucky I'm here, then. I can help you relax,' Tania assured him blithely and Nik's jaw tightened.

Tania Harvey was elegant and blonde, two of the attributes he looked for in a woman, but he freely admitted that he had a low boredom threshold. Her hints that she was hoping for a more permanent place in his life were the last straw. It was time to end the affair—which, if he was honest, had reached its sell-by date even before his trip to Greece.

Close up, Tania wasn't as confident as she appeared. Beneath the glossy façade there were shadows in her eyes, and if he'd had any deep feelings for her he would have felt a tug of compassion. Instead all he felt was irritation with his PA for putting him in an awkward situation. Up until now Kezia Trevellyn had proved to be an excellent assistant, but he didn't need anyone to organise his love-life.

The fleet of limousines lining the drive were evidence that Nik and his guests had already arrived. Kezia parked her Mini and switched on the interior light to inspect her face in the driving mirror. God, she looked a mess, she thought dismally. Her hair had escaped its once neat bun and was tangled around her face; there were streaks of mud on her cheeks and a huge bluish lump on her forehead.

'Prepare for fireworks,' she warned the muddy ball of fur on the seat next to her.

At the sound of her voice the dog cocked one ear and stared at her with soulful eyes. She still wasn't sure if she had actually hit it, or if it had been injured, but to be on the safe side she lifted it into her arms and carried it up the front steps.

'Kezia…my dear.' Mrs Jessop opened the front door and gasped at the sight of Kezia's bedraggled form but Kezia's gaze was drawn to the tall figure whose presence dominated the room.

'*Theos!* What happened to you?' Nik demanded, his face thunderous as he strode towards her.

His expression of utter disbelief would have been comical if Kezia had felt like laughing. Instead, all she could think of was that she had ruined her new shoes and was leaving a trail of mud across the floor. She was so wet that her skirt was plastered to her thighs, and as a final insult there was a huge ladder in her tights.

'I had a slight accident,' she told him briskly, hoping to mask the fact that she felt like bursting into tears. It was delayed shock, she told herself, and had nothing to do with Nik looking as though he would like to strangle her. She hadn't seen him for weeks, and the impact of his exceptional height and broad shoulders encased in a charcoal-grey overcoat made her close her eyes for a second.

He possessed an aura of raw, sexual magnetism—a primal force that was barely concealed beneath the veneer of civilisation his clothes awarded him. Remove the designer suit and the man would still be impressive—probably more so, she acceded faintly as she sought to impose control on her wayward imagination. She had only felt half alive these past few weeks, but now the blood was zinging through her veins. One look from him could reduce her to jelly, and her face burned as she felt his eyes trawl over her mud-spattered clothes. From the gleam of fury in his gaze it was safe to assume that he was not as impressed by the sight of her.

'What kind of accident? What the hell is going on, Kezia? And what is *that?*' he growled as his gaze settled on the animal nestled in her arms.

'It's a dog. It ran into the road and I had to swerve to avoid hitting it. I'm not sure I was entirely successful,' Kezia added worriedly. 'It could be hurt.' She trailed to a halt beneath Nik's impatient glare.

'Never mind the damn dog. Look at the state of you. I expected you to be here, not traipsing around the countryside collecting waifs and strays.' He loomed over her, his brows drawn into a slashing frown that warned of his annoyance, and Kezia felt her temper flare. She had spent all day trying to organise his wretched dinner party, and she hadn't driven ten miles across the Hertfordshire countryside in the pouring rain for fun. 'Mrs Jessop mentioned a problem with the caterers?' he growled.

'There was, but it's sorted,' she said quickly, remembering that she still had to retrieve the boxes of cakes from her car.

'It had better be. I want this presentation to go without a hitch, and I'm relying on you,' Nik warned darkly, his eyes narrowing as he caught sight of the lump on her head. '*Theos,* you're hurt. Why didn't you tell me?' he demanded, pushing her hair back from her forehead to study the large bruise.

Kezia was suddenly acutely aware of an angry glare from Tania Harvey, who had just walked into the room, and she jerked away from him.

'You didn't give me a chance. Leave it, Nik, I'm fine,' she muttered as he probed the lump with surprisingly gentle fingers.

He was too close for comfort. His coat was unbuttoned and she was aware of the muscles of his abdomen visible beneath his silk shirt. He smelled good—fresh and masculine—and the evocative tang of the aftershave he favoured swamped her senses. Her pulse rate soared and she was aware of the need to put some distance between them before she made a fool of herself. Even more of a fool, she amended wryly as she glanced down at her mud-encrusted shoes. That ditch had been full of stagnant water, and she felt her cheeks burn when Nik wrinkled his nose.

'I'll get cleaned up and call a vet,' she assured him.

'For your head?' He was plainly puzzled.

'For the dog. It may have a broken bone, and it must be shocked, it's barely moved.'

'Blow the damn dog,' Nik exploded in a furious whisper, conscious of the need to keep his voice down so as not to alarm his guests. 'I'm going to ring the doctor. You may be suffering from concussion. Something has certainly addled your brain,' he added sarcastically.

'I'm perfectly all right,' Kezia snapped back, refusing to admit that she had a pounding headache. 'I've arranged for Mrs Jessop's niece

Becky and a couple of her friends from the village to help with the party. Becky can show your visitors to their rooms, and we'll meet for cocktails at seven, as planned. Everything's under control, Nik,' she assured him, but he was plainly unconvinced.

'I'm glad you think so. But I'm curious to know what you're going to wear tonight—because you cannot sit through dinner looking and smelling like you do right now.' He let his eyes travel over her disparagingly, unperturbed by her scarlet cheeks. 'You'd better have a bath—you stink—' He broke off as his mistress approached. 'Perhaps Tania can lend you something.'

'I'm not sure Kezia could squeeze into any of *my* clothes; we're very different shapes,' Tania purred, her words drawing attention to her sleek, honed figure compared to Kezia's unfashionable curves.

Kezia gave a bright smile, determined to hide her humiliation and marched towards the stairs leading to the basement kitchen and staff quarters. 'I'll find something,' she promised. 'Trust me, Nik, everything's going to be fine.'

* * *

Twenty minutes later the bundle of mud and fur that Kezia had rescued from the ditch emerged from the kitchen sink, transformed into a small, black dog of dubious parentage.

'It looks like a terrier cross,' Mrs Jessop remarked. 'But crossed with what I couldn't say.'

'He doesn't seem to be hurt, just hungry,' Kezia said, and she sneaked a piece of chicken and fed it to the dog. 'He's very friendly. I'll put a notice up in the village tomorrow. Hopefully someone will come and claim him.'

'I wouldn't bank on it,' the housekeeper told her. 'I reckon he's been abandoned. From the look of him, he's not eaten for days—which doesn't mean you can feed him best chicken breast. That's for dinner, Kezia. I don't think Mr Niarchou would be too happy to hear you've fed the main course to a flea ridden stray.'

'He hasn't got fleas. And now I've bathed him I think he looks rather cute.'

Kezia stroked the dog, and her heart melted when it licked her hand. As a child she had longed for something of her own to love, but the boarding school she had attended from the age of eight hadn't allowed pets. The school holidays had been spent with her parents in Malaysia, where her father had worked. She had pleaded with her mother to be allowed to keep a pet, but her parents enjoyed a busy social life and had had little enough time for their daughter, let alone an animal.

'I can't just turn him out in the rain,' she murmured anxiously. 'Would you mind keeping an eye on him, Mrs Jessop?'

'While I prepare a four-course dinner for fourteen, you mean?' the housekeeper teased good-naturedly.

'I'm sorry about the caterers.' Kezia groaned. 'I can't believe they let me down at the last minute. This presentation is important to Nik, and you know how demanding he is. Everything's got to be perfect. If you can manage the cooking, I'll act as hostess for the evening while Becky and the girls serve dinner.'

'You'll be joining them at the table, though, won't you?' the housekeeper queried.

'No. I'll need to organise wine and drinks, and make sure the evening runs as smoothly as possible. I won't have time to sit down and eat.'

'Nik won't like that,' Mrs Jessop warned, and

Kezia's heart sank as she envisaged Nik's reaction when she failed to join him for dinner.

'He doesn't have a lot of choice,' she muttered grimly. 'The catering company would have sent a master of ceremonies as well as a team of waiters and without them the evening is in danger of being disastrous. We'll just have to manage. We can't do more than our best. But I don't know what I'm going to do about my skirt.'

'Becky has some spare clothes with her,' Mrs Jessop said. 'I'll ask her if she's got anything you can borrow, you're about the same size. But you'd better get a move on if you're going to join them upstairs for cocktails.'

In the shower, Kezia scrubbed her skin until it tingled and she was sure she no longer smelled of ditchwater. She couldn't forget the expression of distaste on Nik's face, and she was determined that when they next met she would be clean and fragrant.

She discovered Becky waiting for her in Mrs Jessop's bedroom.

'My aunt explained about you falling in the ditch. Luckily I've got a spare skirt with me, and shoes. You're welcome to borrow them if they fit,' the young girl offered.

'You're a lifesaver,' Kezia replied gratefully. 'Thanks, Becky. I'll be ready in five minutes.'

The shoes were black stilettos with three-inch heels. Not the style of footwear she would have chosen, Kezia thought grimly, especially when she was going to be on her feet for most of the evening. Mercifully the skirt was a reasonable length—not one of Becky's mini-skirt numbers—but it fitted Kezia like a second skin, the shiny black satin clinging lovingly to her hips and bottom. Teamed with sheer black tights and the high-heels, she looked very different from her usual image of discreet elegance, and she groaned as she imagined Nik's reaction.

A glance at the clock warned her she was running out of time. Taking a deep breath, she headed for the kitchen to see Mrs Jessop, but stopped abruptly at the unexpected sight of Nik chatting to this housekeeper.

'I thought they'd fit,' Mrs Jessop murmured when she entered the steam-filled kitchen. 'Doesn't Kezia look nice, Mr Niarchou?'

'Very…eye-catching.' Nik was leaning against the Aga, his arms folded across his chest.

His eyes narrowed as he focused on her, and Kezia blushed and nervously smoothed an imaginary crease from the skirt. She felt strangely vulnerable without the protection of her formal work suit, especially when Nik's gaze trawled down to her legs and the killer heels.

'I know what you must be thinking,' she faltered, and his brows shot up.

'I sincerely hope you don't,' he drawled. 'I could be arrested.'

'My skirt and shoes are ruined. Becky kindly lent me these. I appreciate they're not ideal…'

'It depends what you're planning to do in them. Lap dancing, perhaps?' he queried sarcastically. 'That should certainly liven up the evening.'

'Look, if you think for one minute that I'm enjoying wearing these clothes, think again,' she snapped furiously.

The glint of amusement and another, indefinable emotion in Nik's eyes was the final straw, and Kezia glared at him. The frisson of sexual awareness between them existed in her mind only, she was sure. He had made it clear that she was just a member of his staff. She must have imagined the flare of heat in his eyes before his lashes fell, concealing his thoughts.

It didn't help that *he* looked so gorgeous, she thought dismally. He had changed into a superbly tailored black dinner suit and a white shirt that emphasised the golden hue of his skin. A lock of black hair fell forward onto his brow, and flecks of amber warmed his dark eyes. She was acutely conscious of him as he strolled towards her. For a man of well over six feet tall, he moved with the lithe grace of a panther— lean, dark and inherently powerful.

She would be able to detect his presence anywhere. He possessed a charisma that alerted her senses and made the fine hairs on the back of her neck stand up. The house had seemed dead without him these past weeks, but now the atmosphere crackled with a surfeit of static electricity that exacerbated her tension.

'How's the head?' he queried, towering over her so that she took a step backwards and banged into the table.

'It's fine; I told you there was nothing to worry about. Contrary to belief, my brain is in perfect working order,' she added coolly and was awarded a look that did strange things to her insides.

Nik laughed, throwing back his head so that her eyes were drawn to the tanned column of his throat. 'I'm glad to hear it, *pedhaki mou.*'

His earlier anger seemed to have disappeared and she quivered beneath the full onslaught of his charm. In many ways he was easier to deal with when he was angry—at least then she could tell herself that she disliked him.

'I called my doctor about signs of possible concussion. Do you feel dizzy?'

She certainly did—but not because she was concussed, Kezia acknowledged ruefully. Standing this close to Nik was making her head spin.

'No,' she answered firmly.

'Nauseous?'

'No.'

'Do you have a headache?'

She hesitated a fraction too long and his eyes narrowed. 'Do you think you were knocked out? Even for a few seconds? And what about your neck? There's a danger you've suffered whiplash.'

'Nik…for heaven's sake!' Kezia stifled a gasp as he caught hold of her chin and tilted her face so that she was forced to stare up at him. 'What are you doing?'

'Checking your pupils,' he murmured, in a low, gravelly voice that brought her flesh out in goosebumps.

She felt as though time ceased to exist. The sounds and smells of the kitchen faded as her senses focused on the man in front of her.

'Curious,' he mused softly, after he had spent what seemed like a lifetime staring down at her.

Kezia fidgeted restlessly, wishing she could break free of the spell that seemed to have frozen her muscles. She wanted to turn her head, but found herself transfixed by his eyes that were the colour of rich sherry.

'What is?' she whispered breathlessly. His description of her as curious made her feel as though he was inspecting a specimen in a jar, and brought her hurtling back to earth.

'I can't decide if your eyes are green or grey, they're an unusual mixture of both. Your pupils are slightly dilated. Why is that, do you suppose?' His breath fanned her cheek, and she swallowed and tried to pull free of his grasp, but he merely tightened his hold.

'I really don't know. But I do know that I feel perfectly all right. It's almost seven, Nik,' she said on a note of desperation. 'We should be upstairs, preparing to greet your guests.'

'In a minute—I want a word with you first.'

A sudden nuance in his voice disturbed her, and she felt a flicker of apprehension. What had she done now? 'I'm sorry about the caterers,' she said quickly. 'But it wasn't my fault—and Mrs Jessop has dinner under control.'

'I'm not concerned with domestic arrangements,' he told her coolly. 'My concern is of a personal nature—our relationship, to be specific, and your apparent desire to be involved in my intimate affairs.'

'What?' The room swayed so alarmingly that Kezia was forced to grip the edge of the table, and she wondered briefly whether she was suffering the effects of concussion after all. 'I don't know what you mean,' she mumbled, her face flaming.

How had he guessed her feelings for him? Had she inadvertently given some sign that revealed her awareness of his brooding sexuality? She couldn't carry on working for him if that was the case. It would be unbearable. Drowning in humiliation, it took a few seconds for her to realise that he was speaking.

'I mean your decision to invite Tania to dinner tonight. Your role as my PA does *not* give you the right to interfere in my private life.'

The amber flecks had disappeared from his eyes, leaving them dark and dispassionate. His concern of a few moments ago had also gone, and she confronted the sickening realisation that his friendliness had been a callous ploy to make her lower her defences while he prepared his attack.

'I didn't invite her. Well, I suppose I did,' Kezia qualified. 'But she knew about the dinner party, and she gave me the impression that you expected her to attend.'

'Did I specify that she should be included on the guest list?'

'No, but—'

'Then why take matters into your own hands? Your job as my PA does *not* require you to organise my love-life.'

'That's not exactly true,' Kezia snapped, irritated by his arrogance. 'It was left to me to dispatch flowers to your last blonde when you ended the affair. *And* I had to pick out a piece of jewellery,' she added, remembering the demeaning trip to the jewellers Nik had sent her on. 'I thought that keeping your harem happy was very much part of my duties.'

'*Theos,* you forget your position, Kezia,' he growled furiously.

She swallowed, and wondered how he could switch from friend to foe so quickly.

'Naturally there may be times when I need you to deal with private matters, but I assumed I could expect a certain amount of discretion. What do you think I pay you such a generous salary for?'

'My staying power?' Kezia suggested sweetly. 'You can't have it both ways, Nik. If Tania is suddenly off the menu, you should have said so.' Her relief that she had misunderstood him earlier, and that he hadn't guessed she was suffering from a massive case of hero-worship, was giving way to anger at his appallingly chauvinistic attitude. He might have the face and body of a Greek god, but he had a heart of stone. She should count herself lucky that he would never view her as anything other than his boring secretary.

'You should be thankful that I had not invited

another…companion for the weekend,' Nik flung at her as he headed for the stairs leading up to the main floor. 'It could have proved highly embarrassing for everyone.'

'But that would have meant two-timing Miss Harvey,' Kezia said slowly, frowning at the implication of his words. His long legs had already propelled him up the stairs, and she raced after him, following him into the drawing room. 'That's a despicable way to behave.'

For a moment she thought he hadn't heard her. He was standing at the bar, his back towards her, but then he turned—and she quailed at the hardness of his expression.

'Let's get one thing straight, Kezia,' he said softly, his tone revealing a degree of cynicism that made her wince. 'How I choose to live my life is my business. In my world, affairs have little to do with the heart, and the women I date know the score. The pursuit of mutual sexual pleasure with no strings,' he elaborated sardonically.

His words made her blush, but inside she felt chilled by his clinical detachment.

His smile was devoid of warmth as his eyes raked over her mercilessly. 'I don't know what

Tania has hinted about our relationship, but she's under a delusion if she thinks she is about to become a permanent feature in my life. I suggest you discount any romantic notions she might have put into your head,' he advised. 'In the unlikely event that I should ever need your advice on my private life, I'll ask for it. Until then I expect you to follow my orders and abide by my decisions without question. Is that clear?'

'As crystal,' Kezia replied curtly.

Beneath his charm he possessed a ruthlessness that made her shiver, but even now she was agonisingly aware of him. Since that day when she had discovered him in her office she had been unable to put him out of her mind. He dominated her fantasies and haunted her dreams. She must have been mad to believe she could work for him, she thought grimly. When she'd learned that she had beaten the many other applicants for the job as his PA she had been filled with a mixture of fear and excitement. It was a dream job, and she had spent the past few months travelling to exotic locations aboard Nik's private jet, but all the while she'd had to fight to hide her attraction to a man who barely noticed her while he worked his way through a variety of elegant blondes.

Voices from the hall warned her that his guests would soon join them, and she struggled for composure. She would rather die than allow him to see her misery—or, even worse, guess the reason for it.

'I think we understand one another perfectly, Nik,' she said coldly, pride giving her the courage to meet his gaze. 'And I can't tell you how glad I am that I'm not part of your world.'

CHAPTER TWO

NIK BIT BACK a retort as his guests filed into the room, but his anger was evident in the rigid tension of his jaw. The words *You're fired* hung in the air and Kezia quickly tore her eyes from his furious face.

She was half tempted to walk out and leave him to it. Let *him* entertain the group of Bulgarian businessmen and their wives—particularly the wives, she thought sourly, noting the way every woman in the room was openly staring at Nik. It wasn't surprising, she conceded bleakly. Despite the fact that all the men present were wealthy and successful—uniform in their formal dinner suits—Nik's height and sheer magnetic presence commanded attention. He teamed sophistication with a raw, masculine sensuality that made him irresistible, and she knew she wasn't the only woman in the room to be fascinated by the idea of taming him.

Another of her fantasies, she reminded herself sharply. Beneath his urbane façade he possessed a wildness that no woman would ever control. Nikos Niarchou answered to no one, and she doubted his glorious arrogance would ever be subdued.

With a sigh, she swung round and came face to face with Tania Harvey, whose late arrival ensured that she was the focal point of attention. In a stunning gold sheath, her blonde hair piled on top of her head, Tania had mastered the art of looking both elegant and sexy, and she smiled confidently as she strolled across the room.

'What on earth has happened to the caterers?' she queried loudly. 'There appears to be a group of teenage girls serving drinks. I would have expected better organisation than this, Kezia.'

'The catering company pulled out at the last minute,' Kezia replied stiffly. 'Becky and her friends kindly offered to help out, and I'm just about to join them in handing round canapés.'

'*You?*' Nik demanded with a frown, and Kezia felt a flash of impatience.

As he had so often pointed out, it was her job

to see that his life ran like clockwork, and if that meant playing the role of waitress at his damn dinner party, so be it.

'Yes—unless you have another suggestion? Mrs Jessop is rushed off her feet, and Becky and the girls can't manage by themselves.' She knew she sounded snappy, but she was tired, her head ached, and she was sure Nik was comparing her appearance in the too-tight skirt with Tania's cool beauty.

He was looking at her now as if she had taken leave of her senses. He wasn't used to being spoken to in that tone of voice, and the hardness of his stare warned her to expect the full force of his anger once they were out of earshot of his guests.

Stifling a groan, she marched over to Becky and her friends, praying they hadn't overheard Tania's tactless remarks. Mrs Jessop had prepared canapés with smoked salmon and caviar to accompany the champagne. Smiling encouragingly at the girls, she picked up a tray and moved among the guests, unaware that Nik's dark gaze followed her.

'Darling, we'll really have to think about hiring more permanent staff,' Tania murmured in Nik's ear, and he stiffened, fighting to control his irritation. 'It's silly to have to rely on the housekeeper and a gaggle of spotty teenagers your secretary has dredged up from the village every time we entertain. And God knows where Kezia gets her dress sense from,' she added disparagingly. 'The skirt she's wearing is indecently tight. Perhaps it wouldn't be a *bad* thing if she spent the evening in the kitchen, out of sight.'

'Tread carefully, *agape mou,*' Nik warned softly, his eyes narrowing as he surveyed her. 'I'm quite happy with my domestic arrangements. I'm sure Kezia is doing her best, in a situation that I understand was out of her control, but if you would prefer not to stay I'll have my driver take you home.'

'I didn't mean—' Tania broke off nervously, her composure slipping. 'You can be so brutal sometimes, Nik. Of course I want to stay.'

'Especially after you went to such lengths to engineer an invitation,' he agreed coolly, feeling nothing but indifference at the tremulous wobble of her mouth. 'You know the rules, Tania. Don't overstep the mark.'

Without awarding his soon to be ex-mistress

another glance, he moved to mingle with his guests, playing the role of genial host while his eyes scanned the room for Kezia.

She had intrigued him from the start, he acknowledged as he watched her work the room, chatting to the guests while serving flutes of champagne. Her intelligence and unflappable nature had made her the ideal choice as personal assistant. Her willingness to put in long hours and travel at a moment's notice were an additional bonus; he had neither the time nor the patience to deal with staff who led complicated private lives.

Kezia Trevellyn had slipped into her role with seamless ease, but he was aware of the sexual chemistry that hovered like a spectre between them. From the moment they'd met at the London office he had been plagued by a burning desire that was as fierce as it was unexpected. Her lush curves were a distraction he could do without, he conceded derisively as his eyes focused on the delightful sway of her bottom beneath its covering of tight satin. The most sensible course of action would be to forget the increasingly erotic fantasies Kezia evoked and concentrate on her excellent organisational skills. One of his unwritten rules was to keep his work and private lives separate, but the physical attraction he felt for her was proving difficult to ignore.

Sensible had never held much appeal, he accepted honestly. He was a man who liked to live dangerously.

As if alerted by some sixth sense, she looked up at that moment and met his gaze. He noted with interest the flush of colour that stained her cheeks as their eyes clashed, and lifted his glass in salute. It was satisfying to realise that the attraction was mutual.

It had been the evening from hell, Kezia decided several hours later as she glanced at the array of dirty glasses that littered the sitting room. Her calf muscles were throbbing almost as much as her head, and with a sigh she sank down onto the sofa.

Fortunately dinner had been a success, thanks to the excellent meal Mrs Jessop had provided and the hard work of Becky and her friends as they'd waited table. Kezia had been kept busy organising the girls, who had been plainly overawed by the elegant formality of the dining room and the number of guests seated around the table. She had taken one look at Nik's glowering expression when he realised she would not be joining the dinner party, and had kept out of his way as much as possible. Luckily the wines she had selected to accompany each dish had seemed to meet with his approval. She'd moved endlessly around the table, refilling glasses, and by the time the party had moved into the sitting room for coffee and liqueurs her feet had been aching and she had longed for her comfortable flat shoes.

Even then there had been no reprieve. Nik had planned a detailed presentation of his ideas for a hotel and leisure complex, a short film and a speech, followed by an opportunity for questions and discussion. There had been no time for Kezia to relax as she had once more assumed the role of hostess, serving drinks to the increasingly raucous group of businessmen, and it had been past midnight before the party finally broke up. Ahead of her loomed a twenty-minute drive through the dark country lanes to her flat, where she hoped to snatch a few hours' sleep before returning to Otterbourne tomorrow.

Sighing wearily, she searched through her handbag for her car keys. They seemed to have disappeared and, muttering an oath, she tipped the contents of her bag onto the coffee table.

'I take it you're looking for these?'

The familiar drawl brought her head up, and she stiffened, each of her senses on high alert, as Nik strolled into the room. He had discarded his tie and exchanged his dinner jacket for one of black leather. She noted the faint stubble visible on his jaw and hastily dropped her gaze. He exuded a brooding sexuality that made her nerves tingle, and she swallowed convulsively, desperate to hide the effect he had on her.

Taking a deep breath, she scooped her belongings back into her bag and walked towards him, her hand outstretched. 'There they are. Where did you find them?' she queried, striving to remain composed when he made no attempt to return the bunch of keys.

'In your bag,' Nik replied calmly, watching the array of emotions that crossed her face—

surprise, confusion, and lastly a flash of anger as the implication of his words hit home.

'How dare you? What do you suppose gives you the right to rummage through my personal belongings?'

'They were on the top,' he informed her hardily. 'And, as to the question of rights, you're my employee, my responsibility, and I have no intention of allowing you to drive home alone this late at night—especially as you were injured earlier this evening.'

'I'm fine.' If she discounted being tired and stressed. She certainly didn't possess the energy to deal with Nik any more tonight. 'It's been a long day and I want to go home.' She glanced pointedly at her watch as she spoke, but Nik continued to study her speculatively while retaining hold of her keys. 'This is ridiculous. You can't hold me here against my will.'

'You should know by now that I can do anything I like,' he said, with his usual breathtaking arrogance. 'It would be better if you stayed the night so that I can keep an eye on you. I still think you should be checked over by a doctor.'

The idea of Nik keeping an eye on her throughout the night was so mind-boggling that Kezia was temporarily speechless. 'There are no rooms spare,' she said quickly. 'And I don't have anything to wear tomorrow—unless you want me to spend the day looking like a lap dancer,' she added tartly, as she recalled his comments on her appearance at the start of the evening. 'One night of humiliation is enough, surely?'

'There was no reason for you to feel embarrassed tonight,' he told her seriously. 'I was impressed with the way you organised dinner. Especially as I understand you had less than twenty-four hours' notice from the catering company announcing that they were pulling out. The presentation went well, and I'm already putting together a consortium of investors interested in backing the project.'

'I was just doing my job,' Kezia muttered, unable to control a surge of pleasure at Nik's approval.

His earlier bad mood seemed to have disappeared, but as far as she was concerned a friendly Nik posed a serious threat to her equilibrium. He was too close for comfort, and despite her best intentions she was unable to drag her gaze from the sensual curve of his mouth. It was definitely time to leave, she thought frantically as she wetted her dry lips with her tongue. The air was heavy with an unspoken tension that was surely the workings of her imagination—but she noted the way Nik's eyes narrowed as he studied her nervous gesture. Her mind ran riot as she envisaged him lowering his head to brush his lips over hers in a slow exploration, and without conscious thought she swayed towards him.

'Are you ready to go?' His voice shattered the sensual haze, and Kezia stepped back abruptly, her face burning.

'I don't need a chauffeur,' she argued stubbornly. 'I'm perfectly capable of driving myself home. Besides, you can't leave your guests.'

'They've all gone to bed,' he said cheerfully, his eyes gleaming with sudden amusement as he studied her pink cheeks.

Had Tania also retired for the night? Kezia wondered. Was Nik's mistress waiting impatiently in the master bedroom, sprawled across the vast bed that she had once glimpsed when Mrs Jessop had given her a tour of the house? And, if so, surely he was keen to join her?

'I refuse to allow you to drive your car until

I've arranged for a mechanic to check it over,' he told her, in a tone that brooked no argument. 'We'll take the Porsche.'

'What about Max? He'll have to come too.'

'Max?' Nik frowned. 'Who the hell's Max?'

'The dog that I almost ran over. I'm going to take him back to my flat.'

'How do you know that's his name?'

'I don't. But I have to call him something until I can return him to his owners. Mrs Jessop thinks he was abandoned, so maybe no one will claim him,' Kezia added, unaware of the wistful note in her voice. She couldn't bear the idea that the dog had been deliberately left by the roadside. 'I'll just run downstairs and collect him,' she said, hurrying out of the room before Nik could argue.

She knew what it was like to feel unwanted, she acknowledged as she scooped the scruffy terrier into her arms. Her heart leapt with pleasure when he burrowed against her, and she was filled with a fierce determination to take care of him. Her mother had always freely admitted she'd never wanted children, and that Kezia's unexpected arrival had been a shock. It wasn't that her parents didn't love her, she conceded, but they had been a professional couple in their forties when she was born, and had expected her to fit into their busy lifestyle. She had spent her childhood feeling that she needed to apologise for her existence, and her years at boarding school, although not unhappy, had reinforced her belief that she was a nuisance her parents didn't quite know how to deal with.

The entrance hall was empty when she carried Max upstairs, but she spied her car keys on the table and for a moment contemplated making her escape. Not a good idea, she accepted ruefully, imagining Nik's fury if she disobeyed him. From experience she knew it was pointless arguing with him when he had his mind set on something. He had made it clear that he intended to drive her home.

But as she waited for him she overheard voices from his study.

'Why do you have to take her home?' Tania's petulant tones were clearly audible through the closed door. 'For God's sake, Nik, I haven't seen you for a month. Why this sudden concern for your secretary? If it weren't so laughable I'd almost believe you've got something going with her. I saw the way you kept looking at her tonight, but I can't imagine what you see in her.'

'*Theos!* Don't be so ridiculous,' came the terse reply. 'She's not my type. But Kezia's an excellent assistant, she's worked hard all night, and it's my duty to see she gets home safely.'

Hastily Kezia stepped away from the door, swamped with misery and humiliation. She already knew she was far from Nik's ideal woman, but to hear him state the fact quite so forcefully was agony. Never in a million years would she allow him to guess how she felt about him, she vowed fiercely. Her cheeks flamed as she recalled the stark disbelief in his voice that he could possibly find his PA attractive. It was obvious he regarded her as part of the furniture, as functional and unexciting as his computer. She must have imagined the exigent chemistry between them; it was just an illusion brought on by her wishful thinking.

She couldn't bring herself to look at him when he joined her in the lobby a few minutes later, and she was silent as she followed him down the front steps. The rain stung her face, but she carefully placed Max on the narrow back seat of the sports car before climbing in next to Nik, wondering how he managed to fit his long legs behind the wheel.

In the confines of the small car he was too close. She caught the subtle tang of his aftershave, and suddenly the heater seemed to be working too well. She was burning up, but balked at the thought of fighting her way through her coat and instead stared stiffly out of the window as he turned out of the drive.

'There was really no need for you to leave Miss Harvey,' she muttered. 'I feel awful for putting you to so much trouble.'

'It's not a problem,' Nik assured her. He sounded disinterested. He was probably counting the minutes until he could join his mistress in bed, she thought bleakly, and fell silent for the rest of the journey.

Driving along the pitch-black country lanes required all Nik's attention, but as they reached the outskirts of the busy market town where she lived he glanced briefly at Kezia. 'Do you live alone?'

The query surprised them both. He'd never shown the slightest interest in her private life before. He had picked her up from home a couple of times, usually when they'd had an early flight, but she had always been waiting for him in the car park and had never invited him in. Did she have a boyfriend? he wondered. Was her lover waiting impatiently for her to return? He was irritated to realise how much he disliked the idea.

'No, I share with a flatmate.'

Her ambiguous answer told him nothing, and pride prevented him from pushing the point. His secretary's love-life was none of his business, he reminded himself impatiently. 'I'll pick you up in the morning,' he informed her coolly.

'There's no need.' Kezia's head jerked round, her consternation evident in her wide eyes. 'I don't want you to have to get up early. What would Miss Harvey say?' she muttered, blushing again as she pictured Nik struggling out of bed after a night of passion with his mistress, in order to collect *her*.

He turned into the small courtyard in front of her flat and cut the engine before turning to face her. 'Why don't you let me worry about the finer details of my private life?' he drawled, in a tone that warned her to mind her own business. 'I'll be here at eight-thirty.'

Kezia opened her mouth to argue, caught the glint in his eyes and thought better of it. 'Fine. Have it your own way. You usually do,' she added under her breath as she climbed out of the car. She had only been trying to help, damn it. She certainly didn't want to pry into his sex life. She lifted Max out of the car and smiled politely. 'Thanks for bringing me home,' she said stiffly, assuming that he would drive straight off, but as she ran up the steps to the communal front door he was right beside her, and she had to crane her neck to look up at him.

'I'll see you up,' he said easily, and her temper, born from a mixture of embarrassment and misery, ignited.

'For heaven's sake, I'm perfectly all right. Miss Harvey will be wondering where you are,' she couldn't resist adding, and was mortified when he glanced down at her, his eyes gleaming with undisguised amusement.

'I've already told you. I'll take care of Tania.'

'I'm sure you will.' She opened the door to her flat and closed her mind to images of just how he would take care of his mistress. 'Goodnight, Nik.'

'Aren't you going to offer me coffee before I

drive back?' He lolled in the doorway, one arm resting on the frame, so that she was aware of the inherent strength of his muscular chest. He exuded a powerful sensuality so intensely male that she rebelled at the thought of him invading her private bolthole. But a voice from behind her took the matter out of her hands.

'Are you coming in or are you going to stand there all night? Oh—hello!' The voice tailed to a breathless whisper, and Kezia sighed as she turned to find that her flatmate Anna was staring at Nik with wide, appreciative eyes. 'You must be Mr Niarchou. Kezia has told me so much about you.'

'Nik, please,' Nik replied in a voice as thick as syrup. He held out his hand and Kezia's impatience intensified. She had witnessed Anna working her magic countless times before, and doubted there was a man on the planet who would prove immune to her beauty. Slender and willowy, her delicate colouring and ash-blonde hair bore testament to her Scandinavian ancestry, while huge blue eyes and a surprisingly impish smile made her simply stunning. They had been best friends since their first day at boarding school, as close as sisters—although right now she could cheerfully strangle her flatmate, Kezia thought grumpily as she watched Nik fall under her spell.

'Are you stopping, Nik?' the pretty blonde murmured. It was an innocent enough query, but Kezia ground her teeth together as Nik gave one of his sexy smiles that made her toes curl.

'I'm not sure. Kezia's still debating whether or not to invite me in for coffee.' His eyes gleamed wickedly as he took in her furious glare, and Anna chuckled.

'Well, I'll make the decision for her,' she said cheerfully, ushering him into the flat. 'I'm Anneliese Christiansen—Kezia's flatmate,' she explained, her blue eyes sparkling, and with a muttered oath Kezia marched down the hallway.

Let Anna entertain him, she thought darkly. She'd had enough of Nik Niarchou for one day. In the kitchen she filled the kettle while Max sniffed around, looking for somewhere to settle. She dug out an old picnic blanket from the utility cupboard and spread it on the floor. If he was going to be here for any length of time she would have to buy him a basket and a lead, she thought happily. He seemed lively enough, but maybe she would take him to a vet, just to make sure he hadn't suffered any injuries when he had run out into the road.

'What on earth is that?' Anna queried as she preceded Nik into the kitchen.

'A dog, of course. What does it look like?'

'A ball of fur on legs,' Anna replied truthfully. 'I suppose it's another stray you've rescued? You know our tenancy agreement prohibits keeping pets in the flat.'

'It'll only be for a couple of days, while I try to trace his owners,' Kezia muttered. 'I could hardly leave him out in the cold. See how thin he is.'

'Kezia's always been the same,' Anna explained to Nik. 'At school she kept a collection of rescued wildlife in the caretaker's shed. Do you remember the time you cared for that injured fox, Kez?'

'Kezia obviously has hidden depths,' Nik murmured, with a curious expression in his eyes that made her blush self-consciously—although she couldn't imagine what he thought those hidden depths were.

'I'm sure you're not interested in reminiscences about our schooldays,' she said stiffly.

He seemed to dominate the small kitchen, and

she wished she didn't find him so unsettling. She couldn't relax, and she envied the way Anna was able to chat so unselfconsciously with him. With a sigh, she left her flatmate to make the coffee and headed for the sanctuary of her bedroom. It was a relief to change out of the borrowed skirt and shoes. Her feet would never be the same again, she thought wryly as she wriggled her toes. Her scalp felt tight with tension, and she freed her hair from its tight knot so that it rippled down her back, all the while trying to ignore the sounds of laughter from the kitchen.

It was ridiculous to feel jealous of Anna, she told herself crossly as she stared at her reflection in the mirror. She was lucky to have good friends, a comfortable flat and a dream job that offered the opportunity to travel the world. It was nobody's fault but her own that she had become fixated with a man who was out of her league. And if she wanted to carry on working for Nik she would have to overcome her fascination for him.

CHAPTER THREE

THE RUMBLE OF NIK'S DEEP VOICE, followed by
Anna's laughter, sounded from the kitchen.
Listening to them, Kezia was tempted to leave
them to it. They appeared to have struck up an
instant accord, she noted sourly. But it had been
good of Nik to bring her home and, much as she
longed to fall into bed, it would be impolite not
to join him for coffee.

Wearily she tugged on jeans and a sweatshirt,
pulled a comb through her hair and padded
barefoot down the hall. The kitchen was empty,
and when she pushed open the living room door
she found Nik alone, sitting in an armchair with
his long legs stretched out in front of him.

'Anna's gone to the flat upstairs,' he explained.
'Apparently your neighbour's suffering some
sort of emotional crisis.'

'Vicky must have broken up with her boy-friend—again,' Kezia murmured awkwardly, feeling strangely disconcerted at being alone in her flat with Nik.

It was ridiculous. They spent hours in each other's company—either in his study at Otterbourne or travelling aboard his private jet—but this was her private space, and his presence unsettled her more than she cared to admit. She was aware of his silent scrutiny and hastily reached for her coffee, burying her nose in the mug and inhaling the tantalising aroma. The caffeine boost eased her nerves, but there would be hell to pay later when it prevented her from sleeping, she acknowledged ruefully.

'Run through the agenda for tomorrow.' His voice cut through the silence, and she gave herself a mental shake.

'I've booked us into the Belvedere Hall Health Spa for the day. There's an excellent golf course—if it's not too wet—plus a gymnasium, and sports facilities for those who want them. We'll have lunch at one, and I've arranged for you to use one of the private conference rooms to continue discussions with the business consortium while I remain with the wives.'

The spa offered numerous relaxation therapies and beauty treatments—although to Kezia the idea of spending the day encased in a mud pack held little appeal, and she was dreading having to strip down to her functional black swimsuit to use the pool. She didn't feel comfortable displaying her generous curves at the best of times, and parading semi-naked in front of Nik was something she'd hoped to avoid at all costs.

Tomorrow promised to be a long day. Today, she amended, glancing at her watch and discovering that it was now one-thirty in the morning. 'Would you like more coffee?' she asked politely, stifling a yawn.

'Thanks, but I think I'd better let you get to bed.' He stood up, and Kezia jumped to her feet, her pulse rate accelerating as he strolled towards her. 'You have beautiful hair,' he murmured, taking her by surprise as he reached out to coil a strand of her long hair around his finger. 'Why do you never wear it down?'

'I can hardly swan around the office like Lady Godiva,' she replied stiffly, finding it impossible to drag her gaze from the chiselled beauty of his face. Nik's puzzled frown cleared as she explained. 'Legend has it that she was a noble-woman who, hundreds of years ago, rode naked through the streets with only her long hair to protect her modesty.'

His brows quirked, and his sudden grin made her heart flip. 'That must have been…chilly,' he drawled. 'But I assure you I wouldn't object, should you want to follow her example.'

She knew he was teasing her, but the knowledge did nothing to ease her tension or lessen her fierce awareness of him. With a determined effort she sidled away from him and headed towards the door. 'I'm sorry, Nik, but I'm dead on my feet and we've another busy day ahead tomorrow.'

'I hope I haven't disrupted your weekend too much?' he murmured as he swung his jacket over his shoulder and followed her into the hall. 'Am I in danger of being thumped by an irate boyfriend for encroaching on your free time?'

'Fortunately I don't have a boyfriend—irate or otherwise,' Kezia replied dryly.

'Really?' His dark eyes trawled over her speculatively, until she squirmed. 'I find that surprising. Why would an attractive woman in her mid-twenties choose to be without a lover?'

Kezia glared at him, twin spots of colour flaring on her cheeks. She felt hot and flustered and thoroughly confused by his sudden curiosity about her private life. For the past three months their relationship had been friendly, but aloof. She wouldn't dream of prying into his personal affairs, and was puzzled by his sudden interest in hers.

'I'm not dating at the moment because I...' She tailed to a halt, unable to reveal that he was the only man who excited her and that anyone else faded into insignificance compared to him.

His ego would love that, she thought grimly as she searched for a suitable excuse for her lack of love-life.

'I was engaged, but it didn't work out, and at the moment I prefer to concentrate on my career. I imagine you've no objections to that?'

'None at all. Your dedication to your job is exemplary,' he said softly, and once again she had the impression that he was laughing at her.

She followed him down the narrow passageway to the front door, and caught her breath when he turned and slid his hand beneath her chin, tilting her head so that she had no option but to look up at him.

'Whose decision was it to end your engagement? Yours or your fiancé's?'

'Again, I can't see what it has to do with you, but it was a mutual agreement. We just felt that we weren't right for each other. Marriage is a serious commitment that shouldn't be rushed into,' she told him, and Nik threw back his head, the sound of his laughter filling the hall.

'My sentiments exactly, *pedhaki mou*—it's good to see we agree on something. I hope your heart wasn't irreparably broken?' he murmured as he stepped onto the landing. 'All work and no play is not good for the soul.'

'I can't imagine how you would know,' she replied tartly, picturing him with the gorgeous Tania. Nik worked and played with equal fervour, and she doubted he had a soul.

He deciphered the play of emotions that crossed her face and grinned unrepentantly. 'Goodnight, Kezia—and thanks for your hard work this evening. My intention is to have the deal signed and sealed by tomorrow evening, and the party are flying home the following morning. What do you have planned for Sunday?'

Kezia shrugged, her confusion evident. He'd just stated that the Bulgarians were leaving on Sunday morning—why would she have planned anything? She was looking forward to a quiet day at home, a chance to catch up on some housework, and maybe taking Max to explore the local park.

'Nothing much,' she admitted.

'Good. Keep it free. I'm taking you to lunch.' He had already reached the stairs and begun his descent.

'But I might have other plans.' He hadn't issued an invitation, it had sounded more like an order, and she rebelled at the thought of him hijacking her one day off.

'You've already admitted that you don't,' he said easily, ignoring her sharp tone.

'I can think of several things I'd rather do in my free time than spend the day discussing your latest business venture.'

'We won't talk about business, I promise.' He had reached the bottom of the first flight of stairs, and as she hung over the banister he smiled up at her, his teeth flashing white against his dark olive skin. 'I think it's time we got to know each other a little better, Kezia, don't you? It'll be interesting to discover if we have anything else in common, apart from our shared views on matrimony.'

He disappeared before she could formulate a reply, but as she walked back into the flat and closed the door Kezia could not throw off her feeling of unease. She didn't know what Nik was playing at, but she had no intention of getting to know him better. Like a cobra, he was safer held at arm's length.

'So that's Nikos Niarchou!' Anna exclaimed when she burst into the flat a few minutes later. 'No wonder you've been so cagey about him.'

'What do you mean by cagey?' Kezia demanded irritably. 'And what's happened with Vicky and Tim now?'

'Nothing.' Anna's momentary frown cleared. 'I said I was going upstairs as an excuse to give you and Nik some privacy. You've never brought him back to the flat before.'

'I didn't bring him back. He insisted on driving me home and, aided by you, invited himself in for coffee. It's nothing to get excited about. And I am *not* cagey about him,' Kezia added firmly.

Anna shrugged, plainly unconcerned by the flash of fire in Kezia's eyes. 'Every time you mention your boss, you blush. But now I've met the gorgeous Nikos in the flesh, so to speak, I'm not surprised you fancy him.'

'I do not fancy him,' Kezia spluttered indignantly. 'I grant that he's attractive, but…'

'He's the sexiest man on the planet,' Anna stated bluntly. 'You'd have to be blind not to notice those brooding come-to-bed eyes of his.' She grinned irrepressibly at the sight of Kezia's scarlet cheeks. 'Is he aware of your feelings?'

'No, he's not…and I don't have feelings for him.' Kezia gave up and muttered something rude under her breath. 'Anyway, he's got a girlfriend. He's going home to her now,' she finished glumly, unable to disguise the bleakness in her voice.

'With his looks he's hardly likely to live like a monk,' Anna pointed out. 'Why don't you let him know you're interested? While I was making the coffee he was definitely grilling me about your love-life. I think you should try flirting with him,' she advised breezily. 'After all, what have you got to lose?'

'Apart from my pride, my self-respect and my job, you mean?' Kezia queried sarcastically.

'What's the real issue here, Kez?' Anna demanded bluntly. 'It's two years since you and Charlie broke up, and I could count on one hand the number of dates you've been on since. Are you going to allow the fact that you can't have children colour the rest of your life?'

'I'm not,' Kezia denied fiercely.

Anna had supported her every step of the way during the illness she had suffered as a teenager, and the bond of trust between them was un-breakable. But, even so, some things were too painful to talk about. At fifteen she had been devastated when she was diagnosed with leu-kaemia. She had fought a long and ultimately successful battle against the disease, and it had only been later, when she'd made a full recovery, that she'd learned the treatment necessary to save her life had wrecked her chances of ever conceiv-ing a child.

'It has nothing to do with me not dating, but there's no escaping the fact that my infertility was a factor in my break-up with Charlie. His parents threatened to cut him out of his inheritance if he married me, so don't tell me it's not an issue.'

'And now you're running scared of getting involved with anyone else?'

'I'm not scared. It's just easier this way. The subject of children, and my inability to have them, isn't a subject I can just drop into the conversation on a first date, is it?'

'I'm not suggesting you go looking for your soul mate,' Anna pointed out. 'If such a thing exists at all, which I doubt. You know my feelings on the myth of happy-ever-after,' she added darkly. 'My dysfunctional family has done little to convince me of the joys of marriage. But that doesn't mean you can't have fun, Kez, and Nik Niarchou doesn't strike me as the kind of man who's desperate to settle down. A passionate fling with a sexy millionaire could be just what you need—as long as you don't do anything stupid like fall in love with him of course.'

Kezia felt her face flame as she sought to avoid her flatmate's intense scrutiny.

'My God! Don't tell me that you've fallen for him?'

'Don't be ridiculous! He's my boss, nothing more. Credit me with some sense, Anna,' Kezia snapped. 'Nik's a notorious playboy. Falling in love with him would be asking for a broken heart, and I intend to keep mine intact, thanks.'

Saturday started badly when Kezia opened her eyes and discovered that her alarm clock had failed to go off. 'Damn and blast,' she muttered as she sped into the shower with less than half an hour to spare before Nik was due to collect her.

She had spent a restless night, due no doubt to the coffee. Her conversation with Anna had reawakened the sadness that continued to haunt her despite her best efforts to concentrate on the future. It was a future that was very different from the life she had dreamed of as a child, she acknowledged bleakly.

Growing up without brothers or sisters, she had decided early on that she wanted a big family. Five or six children at least, she'd confided to Anna. While her friends had planned exciting careers, she'd blithely assumed that marriage and motherhood were her destiny. But her illness had shattered those dreams.

She didn't blame Charlie for ending their engagement, she brooded as she pulled open her wardrobe and searched for something to wear. They had met at university, and from the first she had been honest with him. Charles Pemberton was a future earl, and heir to his family's vast Northumberland estate. Good-looking, and blessed with an easy charm, he'd proved irresistible to a girl who had spent much of her adolescence at an all-girls boarding school or in hospital. But as their relationship had deepened so had Kezia's fears that she would never fit into his aristocratic lifestyle.

Charlie had assured her that her inability to have children made no difference to his feelings for her, but his family had been plainly disapproving of the relationship, and had put pressure on him to end it. Two years ago they had bowed to the inevitable and parted amicably, but Kezia was determined not to make the same mistakes again. She refused to waste her time looking for love and commitment. Fate had dealt her a massive blow, and it had taken her a long time to come to terms with the fact that she would never be a mother. When it had come to the crunch Charlie had realised that he could not accept a future without children, and it was a sacrifice she would not expect from anyone else.

The peal of the doorbell dragged her out of her reverie, and she hastily finished braiding her hair before securing it with an emerald coloured band that matched her jumper. She might have guessed that Nik would be on time and, snatching up her bag, she hurried to greet him.

'Ready?' Nik's gaze skimmed Kezia's appearance, admiring the fluid lines of her cream trousers and the way her lambswool jumper echoed the colour of her eyes.

He was used to seeing her in the formal suits she favoured for work, but he definitely preferred casual, he decided, his eyes narrowing as he noted the way her sweater moulded her full, rounded breasts. For a few seconds he pictured himself exploring those curves with his hands, taking the weight of her breasts in his palms and gently moulding them. To his chagrin heat surged through his body, and he felt an uncomfortable prickling sensation in his groin. Stunned by his reaction, he stepped abruptly away from her, his nostrils flaring.

It didn't help that she was staring at him with those stunning eyes, he thought irritably. He'd never noticed before that her eyelashes were tipped with gold and her creamy skin was flawless. Her only concession to make-up was the touch of pink gloss that emphasised the fullness of her lips, and he was tempted to discover if they lived up to their promise of sensual delight.

'I'll just fetch Max,' Kezia murmured, her pulse leaping at the sight of Nik in designer jeans, a soft grey shirt and leather jacket.

'You're surely not intending to take a dog into a health spa?'

'Of course not. But I can't leave him here alone all day. Anna is flying to the US for several modelling assignments. It's fine, Nik,' she assured him as Max obediently followed her onto the landing. 'Mrs Jessop is going to look after him while we're out. He's very well behaved,' she insisted, when Nik failed to look impressed. 'I can guarantee he won't chew the carpets.'

'He'd better not,' he muttered as he eyed the

scruffy terrier suspiciously. 'What are you going to do if no one claims him? I understand you're not allowed to keep pets in these flats—and he's not living permanently at Otterbourne, so don't even think about it,' he added hardily.

'If it comes to it, I'll just have to move,' Kezia said cheerfully when they reached the car park.

Nik opened the door of his top-of-the-range Porsche and watched in faint disbelief as the dog scrambled over the leather seats and settled comfortably on the back shelf.

'I told you I should have driven my car home last night,' Kezia remarked tartly, correctly interpreting the look of horror in his eyes. The car was Nik's latest toy, his pride and joy, but she refused to leave Max alone in the flat all day; he might feel lonely. 'I'm not going anywhere without him,' she said stubbornly, folding her arms across her chest and wincing as Nik cursed beneath his breath.

'Fine, but if he makes one mark on the upholstery I'll dock it from your wages.'

Fortunately the journey to Otterbourne passed without incident, and Max bounded up the steps of the grand house as if he owned the place.

'He seems to know his way around already,'

Kezia commented admiringly. 'He's so clever. See—he's headed straight for the kitchen. He must feel at home here.'

'Forget it, Kezia,' Nik warned silkily. 'I don't want a dog, and if I did I'd choose an animal that at least *looked* like a dog, rather than a floor mop. Max is your problem, not mine.'

'Your heart really is made of stone, isn't it, Nik?' she said caustically, and was rewarded with a sardonic smile.

'What heart, *pedhaki mou?*'

'I assumed Miss Harvey would be joining us for the day,' Kezia commented an hour later, when the last of their guests finally emerged from the house and climbed into the waiting limousines.

There had been no sight of Tania all morning. Perhaps she was worn out from an energetic night in Nik's bed? Kezia thought cattily, blushing beneath his narrow-eyed scrutiny.

'Tania won't be joining us today, or at any other time in the future,' he informed her coolly. 'And, to satisfy your curiosity, she didn't stay last night either.'

'I'm not curious. It's no business of mine who

you spend your nights with,' she snapped, the colour of her cheeks deepening from pink to scarlet. 'I can't imagine why you think I might be interested,' she added indignantly. 'I'm just your humble secretary.'

'Humble!' Nik gave a shout of laughter as he slid onto the back seat of the limousine next to her and tapped on the glass for the chauffeur to drive on. 'That's not a word I would use to describe you.' His eyes gleamed with amusement as he studied her flushed face, and Kezia pursed her lips.

'I know I'm going to regret asking, but how *would* you describe me?'

'Spirited, strong-willed—a green-eyed wild cat,' he replied instantly, lifting her neat plait into his hand. 'Now that I've seen your hair in all its glory, I'm not surprised. You're a true redhead.'

'And you think the colour of my hair denotes a hot temper?' she queried scathingly. Common sense warned her to drop this conversation now, before it got any more personal, but the imp in her head had scant regard for common sense.

'Actually I find the colour of your hair incredibly sexy.'

Dear God! He was teasing her—wasn't he? She tore her gaze from the indefinable expression in his and stared out of the window, aware that her heart was performing somersaults in her chest. 'You shouldn't say things like that,' she muttered stiffly. 'It's…inappropriate.'

'You would prefer for me to lie?' he queried, his lazy smile doing nothing to settle her nerves.

'I would prefer you to keep your opinions to yourself.' She was intensely aware of his thigh, pressing lightly against hers, and carefully edged along the seat, ignoring his low chuckle that warned he knew exactly how much he unsettled her.

The first time they'd met, in the London office, she had recognised the undercurrent of sexual chemistry that sizzled between them. Her awareness of him had been agonising. She'd felt as though she had been hit by a thunderbolt, and even more unnerving had been the realisation that the attraction was mutual.

It had been with a mixture of excitement and trepidation that she had accepted the post as his PA, but in the three months she'd worked for him she had been secretly disappointed by his purely professional attitude. Obviously she'd been mistaken, she had told herself. Nik wasn't interested in her for any other reason than her secretarial skills, and she must have imagined the flare of desire in his eyes that day. Now, suddenly, she wasn't so sure. She wished she knew what he was thinking—but then again, perhaps it was better that she did not, she acknowledged as she threw him a sideways glance and met his bland smile. Where Nik was concerned, ignorance was definitely the safest option.

The car swung through the gates of Belvedere Hall, and Kezia took a deep breath before turning to face Nik. He was her boss, nothing more, she reminded herself briskly. It was obvious he had finished with Tania, but if he believed she would fill the role of his lover for the day, he was in for a big disappointment.

In fact, she did not see him for most of the day. The rain of the previous night had cleared, to leave a cool but sunny spring day, and he took advantage of the weather to continue his business discussions on the golf course. They met up briefly for lunch, and afterwards the men settled in one of the conference rooms while Kezia and the businessmen's wives made use of the steam room and aromatherapy cave.

She had never felt so pampered in her life, she thought later, as she joined the others by the pool. After a day of such indulgence she should be feeling completely relaxed, but the full massage with a range of essential oils had served only to heighten her tension as she'd fantasised that it was Nik's hands stroking her body. A swim was the only answer, she decided grimly.

The water was cool on her heated skin, and she struck out, completing lap after lap as she sought to ease the fierce tension that her erotic day-dreams had evoked. She could not carry on like this. Somehow she was going to have to get to grips with the overwhelming attraction she felt for Nik before he realised the effect he had on her.

Exhaustion finally overtook her, before she could complete her final lap, and with an effort she hauled herself up the steps at the opposite end of the pool to where she had left her towel.

'Hey, Kezia, are you training for the Olympics?' One of the Bulgarian businessmen sitting at a poolside table smiled as he rose and strolled towards her. He was younger than most of his contemporaries, and good-looking, she supposed—he certainly seemed to think so. She forced a smile as he stepped in front of her.

'I'm just trying to keep in shape,' she replied easily, and then wished she'd kept quiet as his eyes trailed over her.

'You look in pretty good shape to me,' he noted, his insolent grin widening as he studied her pink cheeks.

She'd felt his eyes following her the previous evening, and now stifled a groan when he moved closer and wrapped his towel around her shoulders.

'Here—let me help you dry off. You're freezing,' he said solicitously, and he began to pat her with the towel in a way that was far too personal for her liking.

She was tempted to tell him to get lost, but he was one of Nik's most important clients and she could hardly be rude.

'Thanks, that's very kind of you.'

'You're welcome,' he murmured as he slipped his arm around her waist and drew her over to his table. 'Come and have a drink.'

'Actually, I really must go and get changed.

Nik's probably wondering where I am,' she muttered hastily as she wriggled free of his grip.

'Stop fretting. Your boss is sitting at a table at the far end of the pool. He was watching you while you were swimming. I think he doesn't like you out of his sight for too long,' he added softly, and Kezia followed his gaze, her heart sinking as, even from this distance, she saw Nik's dark frown.

Taking a deep breath, she forced herself to walk around the pool—but as she neared the table where she had left her robe, her steps slowed. Nik was fully dressed, one leg crossed over his thigh in a position of indolent ease, but his watchful stillness warned that he was not as relaxed as he appeared.

For a second she was tempted to turn tail and flee. She felt acutely vulnerable, with her wet swimming costume clinging to her like a second skin. She was so cold that her nipples had hardened to tight buds that strained against the black Lycra, and she longed for the protection of her robe. Steeling herself, she closed the gap between them, daring Nik to comment.

He dared. 'You looked like you were having

fun—although I'm not sure that flirting outra-geously with the male guests really comes under the spec of corporate entertaining,' he drawled, the sardonic amusement in his tone instantly making her want to slap him.

'I was not flirting; I was merely being polite. *He* was the one flirting—with *me,*' she snapped. 'You're sitting on my robe. Can I have it, please? I'm cold.'

'So I see.' His gaze settled unforgivably on her breasts, and to her chagrin she felt them tighten until they ached unbearably. 'Would you like me to help you get dry? You seem happy to allow every other Tom, Dick and Harry the privilege of rubbing you down.'

Kezia took her time, burying her face in her towel and making a show of drying herself while she assembled the correct order of words to tell him exactly what she thought of him.

'That's a vile thing to say. If I'd followed my first instinct I would have pushed him into the damned pool. I wish I had now, and to hell with your precious business deal,' she added furiously.

'I never asked you to prostitute yourself on my behalf,' Nik retorted, the fierce glitter in his eyes warning of the tenuous control he had on his temper.

The unexpected force of his anger surprised her, particularly as she could not understand the reason for it, and tears stung her eyes as she pushed her arms into her robe and tied the belt securely around her waist before replying. 'I didn't think for one minute that you would expect me to prostitute myself. I have more respect for you than that, Nik. It's a pity you don't feel the same about me, instead of jumping to the conclusion that I was leading that man on. How dare you think I was enjoying myself?'

Snatching up her bag, she swept past him. But he was instantly beside her, and caught hold of her wrist to pull her into a quiet corner where they were shielded from view by tall potted ferns.

'Don't walk away from me,' he growled furiously. 'And don't you dare *cry*. How is it that a woman can always resort to tears?'

His impatience was palpable, but Kezia was beyond caring as she fought to free herself from his hold.

Nik stared at her downbent head and inhaled sharply. He was surprised to find his anger draining away. Perhaps it was because Kezia's distress was genuine, rather than a calculated display of emotion, he brooded. All he knew was that the sight of her stunning green eyes glistening with tears was tearing at his insides, and with a muttered imprecation he pulled her into his arms.

'I'm sorry, all right. I'm sorry,' he muttered, struggling with the unfamiliar words of apology. 'I didn't mean to hurt you.'

'Well, you have,' she told him fiercely, scrubbing her face with the back of her hand.

The gesture was strangely child-like, revealing the true extent of her vulnerability and increasing his feeling that he had behaved like an utter bastard.

'I honestly don't know what I've done to make you so angry,' she whispered huskily.

She was staring up at him through her wet lashes and Nik found that he could not drag his gaze from her tremulous mouth.

'I didn't like seeing you with another man,' he admitted slowly, staring down at her with an intensity that made Kezia tremble. 'I didn't like watching you smile at him, and I certainly didn't enjoy the image I had in my head of him kissing you as I know he wanted to do.'

His voice was so low, his accent suddenly so pronounced, that she had to concentrate on his words. His breath was warm on her cold cheek, but as his arms tightened round her she shivered violently. In the background she could hear the sound of voices echoing around the pool, but she was barely aware of them. All she knew was that Nik was holding her, looking at her in a way that sent heat coursing through her veins, and instinct told her it was no longer anger that made his eyes glitter so fiercely.

'Why not?' she whispered, her eyes wide and unblinking as his head lowered.

'Because I wanted to kiss you myself,' he replied with stark honesty.

His lips brushed lightly over hers, warming her. He hesitated fractionally, before increasing the pressure slightly, stifling her low murmur of protest as he initiated a slow exploration. Her resistance was minimal. She had wanted this since the moment she'd first seen him, and heat unfurled in the pit of her stomach. Her lashes drifted down and she parted her lips, the sweep of his tongue so sweetly erotic that she ached to feel him even closer. Her arms crept up to his shoulders, all her senses attuned to the taste of him, the seductive warmth that emanated from his body.

It was heaven, and she would happily spend the rest of her life in his arms, but it couldn't last. This was Nik—a man who only moments before had accused her of making a play for one of his business associates. Her eyes flew open and clashed with his dark gaze. She could see the hint of regret in their depths as he eased back fractionally, grazing his lips gently over hers in one last, lingering caress.

Abruptly Kezia jerked out of his arms and covered her mouth with her hand. 'You shouldn't have done that,' she whispered fiercely, trembling with shock as reaction set in. 'I wasn't leading *anyone* on, and I'm not an easy lay.'

There was genuine amusement in his eyes as he released her and stepped back. 'I'm relieved to hear it, *pedhaki mou*,' he replied softly. 'I prefer a challenge!'

CHAPTER FOUR

KEZIA SPENT THE return journey to Otterbourne House in a state of shock and simmering temper. She couldn't fathom why Nik had kissed her, but it was unlikely that he had been overcome with passion for her, she thought cynically. She remembered all too clearly his categorical denial to Tania that he was attracted to his PA. It was more likely that his sudden interest had resulted from his fiercely competitive streak.

But she had been unable to control her response to him. The feel of his lips on hers had sparked the passion she'd tried so hard to deny for the past few months, and she had kissed him with a fervour bordering on desperation. He must have wondered what had hit him, she thought grimly. Maybe that was the reason he had avoided her for the rest of the afternoon.

The knowledge increased her humiliation, and she longed for the day to be over so that she and Max could go home.

She couldn't bring herself to look at Nik, let alone speak to him, and was grateful that they were sharing the car with some of his guests. When they reached the house she scrambled out of the limousine with more speed than dignity but he caught up with her as she raced up the front steps, his eyes narrowing as she gave a violent shiver.

'Stop running away from me,' he demanded bluntly. 'What's the matter with you anyway? You're as white as a ghost.'

'Nothing. I just don't seem to be able to get warm, that's all.' And if he suggested sharing bodily heat she would hit him, she vowed, dragging her gaze from the sudden gleam of amusement in his.

The guests had disappeared, either upstairs or into the sitting room, and she was painfully conscious that she and Nik were alone for the first time since he had kissed her. She wanted to ask him why he had done it, or perhaps make some flippant remark to prove it had meant nothing to her.

'I'll go and see if Mrs Jessop needs a hand,' she

muttered instead, her nerve failing beneath his dark-eyed scrutiny.

'There's nothing more for you to do here. If you're ready to go home, I'll take you.'

'No,' she replied quickly. 'There's no need. The mechanic said my car's fine.' She was aware of the note of near panic in her voice, but she needed some time out, away from him. She certainly couldn't handle the thought of inviting him up to her flat again. 'I'm not going straight home anyway. I have to go to the store for a few essentials.'

It was only a small lie; she would really go shopping in the morning. All she wanted to do right now was have some time alone. Her head was pounding, and she was aware of a prickling sensation at the back of her throat. The prospect of spending the rest of the weekend suffering from a cold was the last straw she thought dismally as she ran down to the kitchen to collect Max.

By the time she reached home Kezia felt as though someone was driving a pickaxe into her skull. The central heating had been running for a couple of hours, but the flat still felt cold and she turned up the thermostat. Bed was the only remedy if she was coming down with a virus, she decided, as she inspected the empty fridge and gave up on the idea of supper. Tomorrow she would take advantage of the Sunday opening hours to stock up on food for the week—but first, and most importantly, she would phone Nik and tell him she was unavailable for lunch.

Max had settled quite happily on his blanket in the kitchen. Mrs Jessop had allowed him the run of the garden at Otterbourne, and now he curled up into a ball and gave a blissful sigh when Kezia stroked him. Perhaps his owners would see the notices in the village and come to claim before she became too attached to him, she thought. But deep down she had to admit it was already too late. The scruffy mongrel was fast taking up residence in her heart.

She slept through the whole night and woke feeling like death. Sunlight was streaming in through a chink in the curtains, and she could hear Max whining. Gingerly Kezia swung her legs over the side of the bed, and groaned as the room swayed alarmingly. She had definitely picked up a virus and could only hope it would be short-lived; Nik had a punishing schedule booked for the coming week and she didn't have time to be ill.

Somehow she forced herself to pull on jeans and a sweatshirt, and struggled down to the communal gardens to give Max a run. There was something vital she had to do this morning, her brain registered foggily, but by the time she had managed to stagger back upstairs all she could do was collapse on the sofa and fall back to sleep.

Her dreams were fractured and disturbed when from somewhere came an insistent ringing sound that hurt her head, and the distant sound of a dog barking. In her dream she was looking into Nik's eyes, and he was laughing at her as she pleaded with him to kiss her.

'Kezia…wake up!'

Slowly she opened her eyes. Nik was staring down at her, his face grim and unsmiling. He was part of her dream, wasn't he? She shook her head, wincing at the pain that the slightest movement evoked.

'Nik?' She was in her flat, huddled on the sofa and wrapped in the folds of her duvet. Though before she had been frozen, she was now burning up, and with a muttered cry she fought her way out of the heavy cover. 'What…what are you doing here?' she croaked. Her throat felt as though she had swallowed shards of glass, and she tried to moisten her dry lips with her tongue.

'Your neighbour let me in,' he explained quietly. 'I've been ringing the doorbell for the past ten minutes, and almost gave up, but I could hear Max and I was sure you wouldn't have gone out without him.'

Lunch, Kezia remembered. Nik was here to take her to lunch. She had planned to phone him and cancel, but she had forgotten and now it was too late. He was here, looking so devastatingly sexy that, despite feeling so awful, she felt her heart lurch.

He held his palm against her forehead, his touch light and blessedly cool on her heated skin. 'You're running a high temperature. Tell me what feels wrong, exactly?'

'Everything,' she admitted with a faint attempt at humour. 'But it's just a cold, Nik. I'll spend the day sleeping it off and I'll be fine tomorrow, you'll see.'

'Aha.' His tone was plainly disbelieving. 'Drink this.'

The ice-cold water soothed her throat, but could do nothing to ease the aching of every muscle in her body. Weakly she closed her eyes and wished Nik would go. From past experience she knew she must look a mess. Her skin was probably sickly white and her eyes red-rimmed—not an attractive combination. She was sure he meant well, but the sounds he was making as he moved around her flat went straight through her head.

She had drifted into a light sleep when he materialised by her side again, but instead of leaving her in peace he slipped his arms beneath her shoulders and knees and lifted her up.

'What on earth…? Nik? Put me down, please. I'm ill.'

'I'd never have guessed,' came the dry retort. 'Why didn't you say something last night? I would never have let you drive home if I'd known how you felt. I'm taking you back to Otterbourne,' he told her, as he was forced to walk sideways down the narrow hall to prevent her from banging her head on the wall. 'You can't stay here on your own; you look terrible. And before you start arguing, I already know that your flatmate is away.'

'You can't carry me down two flights of stairs,' Kezia muttered feebly, as she fought the urge to give in and lay her head on his shoulder. He was so big, so solid, and already she could feel her muscles relax as she absorbed his warmth. 'You'll break your back,' she mumbled, but he ignored her and carried her down to the car park with impressive ease.

Kezia was vaguely aware of him placing her in the passenger seat of the Porsche, and her senses leapt as she breathed in the scent of his aftershave when he leaned over her to adjust her seatbelt.

'You don't need to go to all this fuss. I can take care of myself,' she whispered, her eyes filling with silly tears at the unexpected tenderness of his smile.

'Humour me, hmm, *pedhaki mou?* I want you where I can keep an eye on you.'

He stowed the bag of essentials he had hastily packed in the boot, and moved round to slide behind the wheel. She was deathly pale, her eyelashes glinting gold on her white cheeks. His mouth tightened at the knowledge that she had spent the night alone and ill in her flat. She could barely stand, let alone take care of herself, he noted grimly, and with a muttered oath he fired the engine and drove off.

Kezia opened her eyes and stared in confusion at her unfamiliar surroundings. She was lying in bed, but it was not her bed, she realised with a frown as her mind creaked into life. The elegant cream walls and rich green velvet curtains were vaguely recognisable. She had been here before—but where was here?

'So, you've finally decided to join the land of the living—about time,' a deeply sensuous voice murmured softly.

'Nik!' She licked her parched lips as she slowly turned her head and found him sitting in an armchair close to the bed.

His long legs were encased in faded denim, his shirt loosely buttoned so that his dark chest hair was clearly visible. With his ruffled hair and the dark stubble shading his jaw he looked markedly different from the urbane business executive she knew, but no less gorgeous.

'At the risk of sounding ridiculous—where am I?' she croaked.

'Otterbourne, in the bedroom adjoining mine.'

'Oh…yes.' Snatches of memory resurfaced— of Nik bundling her into his car, and of feeling so cold that her body had been racked with agonising shivers. She felt masses better, she realised. Her head no longer hurt, and her muscles had stopped aching. 'I told you it was just a cold and that I'd sleep it off. You needn't have brought me here this morning.'

'This morning? You've been here for the last four days—and asleep for most of the time. So it's not surprising you don't remember.'

Feeling slightly stunned, Kezia stared up at the ceiling as she absorbed Nik's words. How could she have been in bed for four days and not realised? Her eyes flew open, and she sat bolt upright as a horrifying thought struck her.

'Max!' If he had been trapped in her flat for four days without food or water, he would surely be dead. 'Nik, I have to go home right now.' She swung her legs out of bed, only to have them placed firmly beneath the covers again. 'Max is all alone…' She slapped ineffectually against Nik's chest, her eyes brimming with tears.

'Calm down. You'll make yourself ill again. The damn dog's here,' he informed her impatiently. 'You don't really think I'd have left him behind, do you? At this moment Max is in the kitchen, waiting for Mrs Jessop to finish cooking his dinner. I believe he's having steak today,' he added sardonically, brushing a tear from her cheek in a surprisingly gentle gesture.

'Thank God,' Kezia breathed fervently as she collapsed back against the pillows. 'Are you sure he's all right?'

'He looks a lot better than you,' Nik told her, with an honesty that made her wince.

She felt hot and sticky, and in desperate need of a shower. Her memory was returning: vague images of strong arms supporting her while a glass of water was held to her lips, and she recalled a soothing voice bidding her to drink, a hand gently stroking her hair from her hot brow. But there were vital gaps in her memory. She couldn't remember changing out of her jeans into her nightdress, and she stared at Nik suspiciously.

'I suppose Mrs Jessop helped to look after me?' She laughed self-consciously. 'I must admit, I don't remember a thing about changing out of my clothes.'

'No, you were pretty well out of it,' he

replied blandly. The gleam in his eyes told her he knew exactly what was bothering her, and she glared at him.

'Are you telling me you took my clothes off?'

'Several times,' he said cheerfully. 'You were running such a high temperature that I've used all the nightclothes I packed for you. But don't worry; they've all been laundered.'

Don't worry! She glared at him, scandalised by the notion that he had stripped her without her even being aware of it.

'I was a perfect gentleman,' he assured her, his grin widening as he took in her scarlet cheeks. 'I left your underwear in place—although I have to admit that those enticing scraps of lace you're wearing sent my temperature soaring almost as high as yours.'

'You're despicable,' she snapped furiously, more unsettled than she cared to admit by the wicked glint in his dark gaze. She was sure he was teasing her, but the knowledge did nothing to quell her quiver of awareness at his potent sexuality.

'I didn't have much choice,' he said, more seriously. 'Mrs Jessop had to take care of her elderly mother for a couple of days. From the sound of it, half the village is ill.'

He leaned back in the chair and stretched his arms above his head, the action lifting his shirt from the waistband of his jeans to reveal the whorls of dark hair that arrowed down over his abdomen. Suddenly the atmosphere in the bedroom seemed way too intimate, and she tore her gaze from him to stare down at the bedcover. Overcome with a weakness that she suspected had little to do with her illness, she closed her eyes and feigned a yawn.

'Sleep now, *pedhaki mou,* and when you wake Mrs Jessop will bring you something to eat. The doctor said you were struck by a particularly virulent virus,' Nik explained as he strolled over to the door. 'It'll be a few days yet until you recover your strength.'

'But what about work?' Kezia murmured anxiously. 'You had meetings in Paris and Cologne this week. How have you managed?'

'I cancelled them,' he said unconcernedly. 'There's nothing so vital that it can't wait until you're better.'

'Right,' she murmured faintly as she absorbed

this startling announcement from a man who possessed the dynamism of a tornado. 'Thank you for taking care of me.' She carefully avoided his gaze as an unbidden image of him undressing her filled her mind. 'I'm sure I'll be back to normal in no time.' She paused fractionally, fearful of sounding ungrateful. 'I'd like to go back to my flat tonight.'

'Not a chance,' he said cheerfully, no trace of regret in his voice. 'You'll stay here until I decide you're well enough to go home. And, just to make sure you're not tempted to disobey me, I'll hang on to these.' He dangled her car keys in the air before slipping them safely in his pocket, and smiled unrepentantly before disappearing out of the door while she was still searching for the words to tell him just what she thought of him.

'I must say you're looking a lot better than you did twenty-four hours ago,' Nik's housekeeper remarked when she entered Kezia's bedroom an hour later. 'I've brought you something to eat. A nice omelette—nothing too heavy.' She placed a tray on Kezia's lap and propped up the pillows. Kezia murmured her thanks, and her face lit up as a familiar figure trotted through the door. 'Max! There you are. I've been so worried about you.'

'I can't imagine why—that dog lives the life of Riley,' Mrs Jessop said with a laugh. 'Mr Niarchou has bought him a collar and new basket, but he's spent every night curled up at the end of your bed.'

'No one's come to claim him, then?' Kezia said, unable to disguise her satisfaction that she would have to hang on to Max for a while longer.

Mrs Jessop shook her head and busied herself with adjusting the bedcovers. Mr Niarchou had instructed her not to say anything about the bullish farmer, Stan Todd, who had turned up at the house demanding the return of his dog. Max had taken one look at him and shot down to the kitchen, where he had later been found cowering beneath the table. He was quite safe now, she had assured the dog. Mr Niarchou had bought him—paid a small fortune for him too. She had overheard the sharp exchange of words between the two men. Stan Todd had a reputation around the village for mistreating his animals, but he wasn't daft. He'd insisted Max was his pride and joy, despite the fact that the dog had been plainly underfed. Mr Niarchou had countered his demands for money with a blistering retort, and had only paid up in return for Stan's assurance that he would make no further claim on Max.

It was funny, Mrs Jessop mused, she'd never thought of Mr Niarchou as a dog lover. But maybe there were other reasons for his change of heart, she realized, as she studied Kezia's delicate features and the riot of red-gold curls spread over the pillows.

'How are you feeling now?' she asked, when Kezia had managed to eat half the omelette. 'That was quite a scare you gave us. Mr Niarchou had the doctor out twice, and he's spent most of the last few days up here with you. He brought his laptop up so that he could carry on working while you were asleep.'

'Did he?' Kezia murmured faintly as she digested this piece of information.

She felt uncomfortable with the idea that Nik had watched her while she slept. It made her feel vulnerable—especially when he featured in so many of her dreams. She just prayed she hadn't called out his name. She was surprised by how tired she still felt, and when Mrs Jessop left she snuggled beneath the duvet and fell back to sleep.

It was dark when she awoke. Someone had switched on the bedside lamp, and when she rolled onto her side she discovered that Nik was back in the armchair, his laptop balanced on his knee.

'You're looking a little better,' he commented when he glanced up and caught her staring at him. 'You've lost that sickly pallor.'

'Thanks!' Kezia grimaced, and wished she could hide beneath the bedcovers, certain that she must look a sight. Nik, on the other hand, looked as though he had stepped from the pages of a male pin-up magazine. His jeans moulded his thighs, leaving little to the imagination, and she sighed and shut her eyes, as if by doing so she could lessen his impact.

'You're bound to feel weak; you've been very unwell,' he said gently.

The virus had hit her hard, he brooded as he switched off his computer. The delicate flush on her cheeks looked a lot healthier than her hectic colour of two nights ago, but she still looked fragile. He had been seriously worried about her—to the point that he had contacted her parents in Malaysia to explain her condition. But, although Jean Trevellyn had expressed both concern and sympathy, he had gained the impression that Kezia was not close to either of her parents. He knew she had no siblings, and it seemed that there were no other relatives in England he could contact—apart from an elderly aunt who lived in a nursing home in Kent.

No wonder she was so fiercely independent, he thought. He couldn't imagine being so alone. His large, noisy, intrusive family back in Greece drove him to distraction, but he had grown up secure in the knowledge that he was adored. Somehow he doubted that Kezia had enjoyed that same feeling of unconditional love, and he was surprised at how protective of her that made him feel. Beneath her prickly exterior he had glimpsed her soft heart and innately generous nature. Her concern for a scruffy stray dog was proof of that. She was a woman who deserved to be loved, and instinct told him she would give her love unselfishly in return.

Where had that disturbing thought come from? he wondered derisively as he uncurled his legs and walked over to the bed. His interest in

Kezia—and he couldn't deny that he *was* interested—was purely physical. The sexual awareness that had simmered since the first time he'd seen her had not lessened in the three months that they had worked closely together. Rather, it had developed to such an extent that he seemed to spend an annoying amount of his time thinking about her. With her fiery hair and lush curves, Kezia Trevellyn was nothing like his usual choice of sophisticated blondes. And he had a feeling that her flashing green eyes spelt trouble. They were witch's eyes, and he was fast falling under her spell.

'So, who's Charlie?' he asked, as he settled comfortably on the edge of the bed—far too close for comfort as far as Kezia was concerned.

'He was my fiancé,' she replied, looking puzzled. 'Why do you ask?'

'You were calling out his name in your sleep. You seemed upset,' he added softly. 'It's said that our dreams reveal our innermost hopes and desires. Perhaps deep down you regret ending your engagement more than you realize?'

'I don't. Of course I don't,' Kezia replied quickly. She had no idea why she had called for

Charlie, and she shuddered to think of the hopes and desires she might have inadvertently revealed to Nik while she was asleep. 'Er...did I mention anyone else?'

'You didn't give a list of past lovers,' he said dryly.

'That's because there isn't a list. Only Charlie.'

'Do you mean that he was your first long-term relationship?'

'First and last,' she quipped flippantly. 'When we broke up I decided that I don't want to be tied down. I'm not looking for love and commitment. I enjoy my independence too much.'

'And yet you still dream of him? Perhaps you were more affected by the split than you care to admit?' Nik suggested. 'Did you love him?'

'Yes,' she said honestly. 'But there were reasons why our marriage would never have worked.'

Reasons that were far too painful to reveal, she thought bleakly. Her infertility was a secret sadness she had only shared with her closest friends. There was no reason for Nik to know.

'I can't believe how much better I feel,' she said brightly, desperate to alter the course of this conversation, which was becoming too personal.

She didn't understand Nik's sudden interest in her private life, and found it unsettling. Maybe he was bored with being cooped up in the house with her for days—or possibly he was regretting ending his relationship with Tania. She couldn't forget the way he had kissed her at the spa, but now she wondered if she had imagined it. Perhaps it had been a figment of her fevered dreams while she was ill. Yet the feel of his lips on hers, the taste of him, lingered in her mind.

'I'd like to have a shower,' she said firmly, hoping he would take the hint and go away.

He studied her speculatively for several minutes, his eyes hooded beneath heavy lids so that she had no idea of his thoughts. 'If you're sure you feel up to it, you can use my bathroom—but I'll be waiting outside, and you're not to lock the door. I want you to promise you'll call me if you feel dizzy or faint.'

Some chance! 'Of course,' she assured him innocently. The thought of him storming into the bathroom while she was taking a shower was enough to make her head spin, and she was grateful for the arm he slipped around her waist as he supported her.

She had been sleeping in the small dressing room adjoining the master bedroom, and as he led her through to the *en-suite* bathroom she quickly averted her gaze from the magnificent four-poster bed that dominated his room.

It was a room designed for seduction, she thought weakly as her heart-rate accelerated. The pale, neutral coloured walls provided a backdrop for rich burgundy velvet curtains that matched the drapes around the bed. The satin bedspread had been thrown back to reveal cream silk sheets, and the pillows still bore the indentation of his head. Her imagination went into overdrive as she pictured his naked body stretched out on the silk, his handsome face relaxed in sleep while impossibly long black lashes feathered his cheeks.

'Excuse the mess. I'm not the world's tidiest man,' he confessed with a complete lack of contrition as she stepped over a black silk robe that was lying in a heap in the middle of the floor. 'My mother insists that I need to find a wife—God forbid!' His mouth curved into a smile that pierced her soul. 'Like you, I value my independence.'

His eyes skimmed the silvery grey chemise that he had helped her into some time during the previous night. She had been so hot that he'd had no option but to change her nightclothes yet again. It was lucky that when he had gone to her flat and found her ill he had simply scooped up the contents of her underwear drawer and flung them in a bag. True, the tiny grey wisp of satin could hardly be described as practical, he conceded, but it was the only clean thing she'd had left. He found himself wondering what she'd had in mind when she'd bought it—or, more pertinently—who. It certainly hadn't been designed to sleep in, he thought cynically as his gaze settled on the delectable fullness of her breasts revealed by the low-cut neckline.

Had she bought it to please her fiancé? Had Charlie once unfastened those ribbon straps and drawn the gossamer silk down so that her breasts spilled in creamy abundance into his hands? His displeasure at the thought was intense, and his mouth tightened. He had never experienced jealousy in his life, and had no reason to suppose that the burning feeling in the pit of his stomach now was anything other than indigestion. But that didn't explain why he was filled with such a violent dislike of a man he had never even met.

Kezia was fast becoming a complication in his life that he could no longer ignore, he mused, as his gaze settled on the red-gold curls that tumbled over her shoulders. She'd barely eaten a thing for the past few days, and her cheeks looked hollow, but fortunately she still retained her gorgeous sexy curves, he noted as his eyes trailed over her hips. She had a body that would tempt a saint—as he had discovered when he'd cared for her during her illness. While she had been unwell he had steeled himself to ignore the temptation her semi-naked body posed, but now she was better and his good intentions were slipping.

Experience warned him of the dangers of mixing work with pleasure. Ordinarily he would not have contemplated an affair with a member of his staff who had proved herself to be such an excellent PA. But these were no ordinary circumstances, he acceded derisively. He had never wanted anyone as fiercely as he wanted Kezia. Not since he was a teenager, when he had been fixated with a glamorous thirty-something Greek actress had he been held at the mercy of his hormones. He couldn't look at Kezia without remembering how it had felt to kiss her and wanting to do it again. And what was to stop him? he asked himself as he ushered her into the bathroom. She wasn't immune to him. Her response when he had kissed her had been unexpectedly passionate. And even now he was aware of her tension, of the slight tremor of her hand as she pushed her hair out of her eyes, telling him she was not as self-assured as she would have had him believe.

'There's fresh towels in the cupboard. Call me if you need anything,' he bade with a smile, as she stared at him with her stunning eyes. 'Unless you'd like me to stay and help?' he added, enjoying the way her cheeks flooded with colour.

'I can manage, thanks,' she said stiffly.

Definitely not immune, he noted with a surge of satisfaction. Her pupils were dilated, her lips slightly parted, and he knew she was as aware of the exigent chemistry that simmered between them as he. What harm could there be in allowing their mutual attraction to develop into a full-blown sexual relationship? Kezia had already stated that she enjoyed her independence. She wasn't looking for commitment any more than he was. They could indulge in an affair, confident that neither had expectations of it leading to anything more permanent.

It really was an ideal situation, Nik decided as he closed the bathroom door and stretched out on his bed while he waited for her to finish her shower. It made perfect sense for Kezia to fill the dual roles of his PA and mistress. There would be no annoying separations while he was away on business, because as his assistant she'd always travel with him, and as his lover they would spend their nights together as well as the days.

And when they decided, some time in the future, that the relationship had run its course, she could return to being his PA. She was good at her job, and he didn't want to lose her—but he wouldn't need to. She had told him she wasn't looking for love. When their affair ended she would presumably be happy to continue with her career, and there would be no bad feelings or messy recriminations.

All he had to do was convince her that an affair was the logical solution to the fierce attraction that burned between them. And, without wanting to be over-confident, he didn't anticipate too many difficulties on that score. Persuading his numerous lovers into his bed had never proved a problem—his wealth had helped with that, he conceded with a degree of self-derision. And, in addition to the Niarchou fortune, he had been blessed with a face and body that acted like a magnet to women of all ages.

But Kezia was different from the usual brittle sophisticates he dated. She might not be looking for love, but he doubted she was the type to participate in a string of casual sexual encounters. She had admitted that her fiancé had been her only serious boyfriend, and although he was certain that she was attracted to him, she seemed determined to fight her feelings.

If he wanted Kezia, he would have to woo her, Nik brooded. He would have to take his time, persuade her with all the subtle means at his disposal of the benefits of having an affair with him. He had gained the distinct impression from his conversation with her mother that there had been little fun in her life. He would wine her and dine her. He would lavish his attention on her until he broke her resistance.

The bathroom door opened and she stepped hesitantly into his bedroom. Her hair fell in damp tendrils around her face so that she looked young and infinitely vulnerable, and Nik felt something tug at his heart. He was impatient to make love to her—every instinct told him that sex with her would be mind-blowing—but first he would have to win her trust. It was a long time since he'd had to try at anything, and as he smiled at her he was filled with a sense of anticipation. She would be worth the wait.

CHAPTER FIVE

IT WAS LATE when Kezia followed Nik out of the restaurant and over to his car. Dinner at an exclusive London hotel had been out of this world, she mused, remembering the rich chocolate mousse that she had been unable to resist. She would regret the extra calories tomorrow—along with the two glasses of champagne Nik had tempted her to. As the evening had progressed she had begun to feel relaxed, and the tiniest bit light-headed—which presumably had been his intention. He had been buttering her up before he dropped his bombshell.

'I don't want to go on a cruise,' she argued now, for the twentieth time, as he negotiated the busy London traffic. 'I don't like boats and I get seasick on a pedalo.'

'You won't feel sick on the *Atlanta,*' Nik assured her calmly. 'She's the pride of the

Niarchou fleet—a luxury liner that has just undergone a multimillion-pound refit.'

'Well, I still don't like the idea of spending three weeks at sea.'

Any more than she relished the thought of spending three weeks cooped up on a boat with Nik, with no chance of escape, she thought dismally. It was two weeks since he had taken care of her while she was ill, and in that time she had detected a subtle shift in their relationship. The sexual awareness that had simmered beneath the surface was more intense, and she could no longer blame the fierce tension between them on her imagination.

Nik wanted her. She was aware of the barely concealed hunger in his eyes when they trailed slowly over her, hovered longer than they should on her breasts, before moving up to stare at her broodingly, as if he was looking for an answer to the unspoken question that hung over them. The question that occupied her mind to the exclusion of virtually everything else. What, if anything, was she going to do about their undeniable attraction for each other? Ignore it, seemed the most sensible option. She understood now why ostriches stuck their heads in the sand. Part of her wished she could hide away until Nik's interest in her had cooled—as it surely would. He freely admitted he had a low boredom threshold, and she knew that any kind of relationship between them would be brief and designated almost exclusively to the bedroom.

The thought should have shocked her, but far more shocking were the explicit images that filled her mind of Nik's naked body entwined with hers as he made love to her on his huge four-poster bed. Common sense warned that he only wanted her for one thing, and that when their affair ended it would also probably spell the end of her job. She couldn't blithely carry on working as his PA while he moved on to his next mistress; it would tear her apart. And therein lay her problem, she acknowledged heavily. She had sympathised with Charlie's reasons for ending their engagement, but it had still hurt, and she'd vowed never to make herself so vulnerable again. She had no intention of falling in love with Nik, but some deeply buried instinct for self-preservation warned against surrendering to the desire that burned between them. It would be playing with fire, and she was afraid of getting burned.

Twenty minutes later he swung the Porsche into the parking area outside her flat and cut the engine. Would he expect her to invite him up for coffee? She glanced at him, and felt her heart lurch as her gaze clashed with his in the dim interior of the car. The evening had been wonderful, despite the fact that she had felt on tenterhooks most of the time.

They had attended a show at the London Palladium before dinner. The musical had won rave reviews, and tickets had been sold out months in advance, but Nik had seemingly had no problem in booking a private box. Helping him to entertain clients was one of her duties, he had pointed out when she had initially declined his invitation. And so it had been with a mixture of reluctance and feverish anticipation that she had slipped into an elegant black evening dress and paced her flat until it was time for him to collect her.

He had waited until they'd arrived at the theatre before revealing that his clients had been forced to cancel at the last minute. But there was no reason why *they* should not enjoy the show, he'd murmured persuasively, awarding her one of his sexy smiles that made her go weak at the knees.

Sitting with him in the intimacy of the private box, she had been acutely aware of the formidable width of his shoulders, the slight pressure of his thigh pressed against hers, and she had barely been able to concentrate on the stage below. Her senses had been finely tuned to every breath he took, every slight movement he made, until she had felt suffocated by his presence. For one mad moment she'd wondered how he would react if she turned her head and pressed her mouth against the tanned column of his throat visible above the collar of his shirt…

Get a grip, she told herself crossly, as she dragged her mind back to the present and released her seatbelt. She was a twenty-four-year-old professional career woman, not a teenager at the mercy of rampaging hormones. She could handle Nik's presence in her flat for half an hour—and besides, there was still the subject of the cruise to discuss. And, more pertinently, her determination not to accompany him on it.

'Would you like to come up for coffee?' she murmured as she opened the car door.

'I thought you'd never ask,' he drawled sardonically, and she blushed as she belatedly realised how long they had been sitting in the car.

Max greeted her joyously, wagging his tail ferociously—although fortunately he seemed to understand her pleas not to bark. It was growing increasingly difficult to smuggle him in and out of the flat, past the prying eyes of the caretaker who lived on the ground floor, and Max's future was another problem looming on Kezia's horizon.

Nik had told her he'd managed to trace the dog's owners and discovered that they were no longer able to care for him. Max was her responsibility. She refused to countenance the idea of taking him to a dog pound, and he was another very good reason why she couldn't spend the next three weeks cruising around the Mediterranean.

'He can stay at Otterbourne. I've already checked with Mrs Jessop and she's quite happy to take care of him,' Nik assured her blandly when she brought up the subject of Max.

'But I don't want to leave him for all that

time,' she muttered, unable to disguise her disgruntled tone as her foolproof excuse for staying on dry land disappeared. 'He might forget me.'

'I doubt it. You're not easily forgettable,' Nik told her silkily, the sudden gleam in his eyes setting her nerves on high alert.

He had followed her into the kitchen and dominated the room as she moved between the worktop and the fridge to collect milk for the coffee. She wished he would go and sit down in the living room, she thought as she was forced to squeeze past him.

His trip aboard the *Atlanta* had been scheduled in his diary for weeks. The first voyage of the Niarchou Group's newly refitted cruise liner was being promoted as the trip of a lifetime, offering unequalled luxury for those fortunate enough to be able to afford it. As company chairman, it was not surprising that Nik had decided to join the ship for its first sailing—but it hadn't occurred to her that he would expect her to accompany him. She had viewed the three weeks that he would be away as a much-needed breathing space, a chance to get a grip on her wayward emotions and she was dismayed by her secret thrill of anticipation at the thought of travelling with him

'Surely it would be better if I stayed behind to run your office?' she argued valiantly. 'You don't need me with you while you're sunning yourself around the pool—unless my duties now include applying sunscreen to your back, of course.'

'I'll have it written into your contract,' he said, with a wicked grin that made her blush. 'I need you with me because this is a working trip. Not a holiday.'

'I see.' Kezia sniffed.

Work was safe; she could handle him if they stuck to their roles of employer and assistant. Her fear had been that since he hadn't yet replaced Tania in his bed he might expect her to fill in as his mistress. But of course there would be a queue of nubile blondes on board only too eager to offer their services in that department, she acknowledged grimly.

'I suppose I'd better get myself organized, then,' she said grudgingly. 'The ship sails next week. That doesn't leave me much time to pack.' Especially as she would need to fit in a couple of shopping trips before they left. The weather in England was unseasonably cold for late spring, and she was still wearing her winter boots and coat, but the temperatures in the Med would require a variety of summer outfits. 'I may need to take a day's leave during the week,' she murmured.

'No problem. You'll have to rearrange my diary anyway. I'm returning to Greece for a few days, but I'll be back in time to join you on the ship when it sets sail from Southampton.'

His smile faded, and she had the impression that his thoughts were suddenly miles away. She turned her attention to the task in hand and added a spoonful of sugar to his coffee, but no milk. In many ways he was a stranger to her, and yet she knew so many intimate details about him—how he took his coffee, the fact that he liked his steak rare and preferred red wine over white. She had become adept at reading his moods too, and although the expression in his eyes was unfathomable, she knew something was troubling him.

'Is something wrong at home?' she queried softly, aware that, wherever he settled in the world, the small Greek island in the Aegean Sea where he had spent his childhood was where his heart lay.

'My father's in hospital.' He took a gulp of his coffee and stared down at the cup, as if debating whether to elaborate further. 'He fell and broke his hip a couple of months ago, and it's not healing as well as it should. Now he has an infection and may need surgery.'

'I'm sorry. You must be worried about him,' Kezia murmured gently, instinctively reaching out to put her hand on Nik's arm. Although he frequently bemoaned the fact that his large family drove him crazy, he plainly adored his parents, as well as his four sisters and a multitude of nieces and nephews, but she guessed that he was especially close to his father. 'This must be a difficult time for all of you.'

Nik shrugged and carefully avoided her gaze. It was a telling gesture from a man who was perceived by most to be invulnerable, and her heart ached for him. 'He's eighty, his bones are brittle, and he has a weak heart,' he admitted gruffly. 'But he insists he's sticking around until I've settled down and produced the next Niarchou heir—so no pressure,' he quipped dryly.

'You're their only son, so I suppose your parents are keen for you to have children one day,' Kezia said quietly, wondering why her heart felt as though it was splintering.

'My mother in particular is obsessed with the idea that I must continue the Niarchou line,' he agreed ruefully. 'Every time I go home I'm presented with a selection of nice Greek girls who she's deemed suitable wife material.'

'Poor you!' Her sarcasm disguised the ridiculous urge to burst into tears and she lifted her hand from his arm, but as she did so he captured her fingers and entwined them with his.

'As I've already mentioned, I've no desire to investigate the joys of matrimony. Certainly not at the moment,' he drawled, the glimmer of amusement in his eyes fading as he studied the delicate beauty of her upturned face. 'I like my life the way it is: uncluttered, uncomplicated, and full of interesting possibilities.'

Without her being aware of it, he had moved closer so that she was trapped against the worktop, her fingers still caught in his grasp. A gentle tug was all that was necessary to draw her up against his chest, and as her lashes flew open she felt her heart lurch at the burning heat of his gaze. The sudden tension in her small kitchen was tangible, and a shiver of excitement ran the length of her spine.

'Nik…don't,' she pleaded, watching with wide-eyed fascination as his dark head slowly lowered. His mouth was millimetres from hers, a sensual temptation she knew she should resist, but her will-power had deserted her and only a fierce, elemental hunger remained. Nervously she moistened her lips with the tip of her tongue, and his eyes narrowed on the frantic movement.

'Don't what? Don't do this?' He brushed his lips lightly over hers, tasting her with delicate precision that left her aching for more. 'I can't help it, *pedhaki mou.* I wanted to kiss you senseless the first time I saw you. We'd met barely five minutes before, yet that day in the London office I wanted to rip your blouse from your shoulders and ravish you. And you wanted it too,' he added softly, capturing her gasp of denial with his mouth.

This time his lips were firmer, demanding her response as he deepened the kiss to a level that was unashamedly erotic. With a sigh she opened her mouth, so that his tongue could make an intimate exploration that left her trembling with need. She could no longer deny him or herself, and her arms crept up around his neck to hold him to his task. The movement brought her body up hard against his, and she revelled in the feel of every muscle and sinew pushing into her soft curves.

'I don't know how I've kept my hands off you for so long,' he admitted thickly. 'Especially since I cared for you during your illness and discovered the gorgeous sexy curves that you keep hidden beneath your prim suits. The temptation of your near naked body drove me almost to distraction, but you were unwell and I could do nothing to assuage my desperate need to make love to you.'

As he spoke he slid one hand into her hair to hold her still while the other roamed down to her bottom, back over her hip and up, to discover the dip of her waist and above it the generous fullness of her breasts.

'You have a body to *die* for, Kezia,' he groaned, his voice velvet-soft as he rolled each syllable of her name on his tongue.

He trailed a line of kisses down her neck and then lower still, following the neckline of her dress to the valley between her breasts. Kezia held her breath as he cupped one soft mound in his hand, took the weight of it and gently kneaded her flesh through the barrier of her dress. She wanted more, wanted to feel his hands on her skin, and she released her breath on a low moan of pleasure when he eased his fingers beneath the material to caress her. Her nipple had hardened to a tight bud that throbbed unbearably when he brushed his thumb pad across it. Heat coursed through her so that she strained closer to him, no thought in her mind but her desperate need for him to continue his sensual magic.

She felt bereft when he released her breast, and muttered her disapproval against his mouth. But he smiled and slid his hand down to caress her bottom with slow circular movements that forced her thighs into close contact with the hard proof of his arousal. It should have shocked her, but instead she felt a surge of triumph that he wanted her so badly, and clung to him as he rocked his hips against her.

'Desperate as I am to make love to you, I'm not sure that your kitchen table is big enough for what I have in mind—or sturdy enough,' he murmured in her ear, his voice tinged with a hint of amusement that brought her skidding to a halt. 'I'm sure we'll be a lot more comfortable in your bedroom.'

What in heaven's name was she doing? Her lashes flew upwards, and she stared at him in a mixture of bewilderment and growing shame. His eyes were hooded, but nothing could hide the gleam of fierce desire in their depths. Nik was hungry for her, and for a few scandalous seconds she was tempted to blank out the whispered warning in her head and lead the way to her bedroom. She wanted to feel him skin on skin, to glory in the touch of his hands on her naked body and enjoy the exquisite pleasure of his mouth caressing every inch of her.

So much for her vow to ignore her overwhelming attraction for him, she thought derisively. She had melted at the first touch of his lips on hers, and even now her body was trembling with the urgent desire to remain in his arms. Fortunately her brain outvoted her body as it struggled to make sense of her uninhibited response to him, and she jerked clumsily out of his grasp, dismayed to see how eagerly her breasts were straining against the silky material of her dress.

He was watching her silently, like a predator waiting for the right moment to strike, but he made no move to prevent her from stepping away from him. Kezia gripped the edge of the worktop and forced oxygen into her lungs.

'Nik, we can't…this was…'

'A mistake?' he suggested softly. 'The result of too much champagne?' You can do better than that, *pedhaki mou*. We both know this has been brewing since the first time we met. But—' he shrugged indolently, his mouth curving into a smile that was wickedly sensual '—I agree. It's too much, too soon. We have plenty of time.' He seemed wholly satisfied at the thought, and his confidence shook her.

Plenty of time for what, exactly? she wondered as panic swamped her. Nik plainly assumed that she was his for the taking, and her response to him tonight had surely added fuel to that belief, she acknowledged grimly. How could she convince him that she had no intention of ever sharing his bed? How could she convince herself?

She sensed rather than saw him move, and her muscles tensed as she prepared to reject him. But he made no attempt to touch her, and instead reached into his jacket.

'This is for you,' he said, as he took a plastic

card from the selection in his wallet. 'I've taken it out in your name so that you can go on a shopping spree in preparation for the cruise.'

Kezia stared at him blankly while her brain assimilated his words. 'I can afford to buy my own clothes, thank you,' she replied stiffly.

'Of course.' He gave a careless shrug. 'But the trip will require more than your usual choice of workwear, and I don't expect you to have to foot the bill for designer evening dresses.' He held out the card and frowned when she made no move to take it from his fingers. 'Enjoy it, Kezia,' he murmured indolently. 'It's not every day that you're given the opportunity to shop in Bond Street. I'm looking forward to seeing you in clothes that show off your gorgeous figure. Choose outfits to please me…hmm, *agape mou?*'

'I am not your lover,' she choked, outrage and blinding fury filling her in equal measures.

Her grasp of Greek was limited, but there was no mistaking the meaning of his words. His eyes slid over her in insolent appraisal, as if he was mentally stripping her, and she felt sick with shame. Her role in his life was purely on a professional level, and she would *not* allow him to

treat her as a sultan would his favourite concu-
bine, clothing her in fine silks for his delectation.

'I'm your personal assistant, Nik. Not your
whore,' she snapped icily. 'I'm afraid you're
mistaken if you think that what happened tonight
was a prelude to three weeks of sun, sea and sex
while we're stuck on your damn ship. You said it
was a working trip,' she reminded him, when he
said nothing, just stared at her in stunned silence—
although the glitter in his eyes warned of his anger.
'I'll be accompanying you as your PA, nothing
more. My working hours are nine to five, and just
because we'll happen to be in the middle of the
Mediterranean, I see no reason why that should
change. I certainly won't be swanning around in
designer gowns, playing the role of your mistress.'

For a moment she thought he would explode.
His face was a taut mask, the skin stretched tight
over his sharp cheekbones, his jaw rigid as he
fought to control his temper. 'Perhaps I should
remind you that your working hours are entirely
at my discretion?' he said in a clipped tone. 'I
expect you to be at my beck and call whenever
I require your…services,' he added silkily, his
mouth curling into a contemptuous smile as he

studied her scarlet cheeks. 'I also expect you to be suitably dressed to dine with the exclusive clientele who have chosen to travel aboard a Niarchou ship. See to it that you don't disappoint me, Kezia.'

He flung the credit card onto the table and stalked out of the kitchen without awarding her another glance. Kezia had never seen him so angry, and her heart was thumping as she followed him down the passage to the front door.

Maybe she had misjudged him? As a representative of the Niarchou Group, it *was* her duty to look and act the part of the chairman's PA, she conceded with a groan. Nik's offer for her to charge the clothes that would be a necessary part of her job to the company account had not been a ploy to persuade her into his bed. It had been an act of kindness that she had flung in his face—and now he was going, storming out of her flat in a furious temper to race to the bedside of his ill father.

'Nik, I'm so sorry.'

He had already flung open the door, but halted and spun round to face her, flicking her a glance of such disdain that she shrivelled.

'I think I may have been mistaken about the

reasons behind your offer. I didn't mean to be insulting.'

'God forbid that you should ever try,' he snapped sarcastically, reining in his impatience at the look of misery in her eyes. 'I see nothing wrong with admitting to feelings of sexual desire, Kezia. It's not a crime. You're an incredibly beautiful woman, and I'm quite honest about the fact that I'm attracted to you—as I suspect you are to me. We're two consenting, uncommitted adults,' he pointed out coolly. 'Why shouldn't we spend the night together?

'I can think of at least a dozen reasons,' she said tightly. 'Number one being that I don't do casual sex.'

'And yet you've already told me that since your engagement ended you've not been looking for a long-term relationship? So, what do you do to appease the natural physical desires of a healthy young woman, Kezia?' His eyes moved over her flushed face, and she detected a hint of amusement in his dark gaze.

'I don't have any desires. Physical or otherwise,' she muttered icily, her temper flaring when he threw back his head and laughed.

'Now I know you're lying, *pedhaki mou*. The way you come alive in my arms is proof of that. You are the most sensually responsive woman I've ever met, and I'm genuinely interested to know why you're so desperate to deny yourself the joy of sexual pleasure. Perhaps your parents indoctrinated you with strong morals?' he murmured, almost to himself. 'Did you learn somewhere in your upbringing that sex is a sin?'

Oh, God! She couldn't be having this conversation, Kezia thought frantically as anger and embarrassment fought against the insidious voice in her head that whispered Nik had a point. Why couldn't she be more relaxed and simply go with the flow? She wanted Nik, it would be a lie to deny it, and he'd made it clear that he found her attractive. There was no reason for her to turn down a night of passion with him other than fear—not of him, but of herself. She simply did not have the courage to give her body and still retain control of her heart when, for her, the two were inextricably linked.

'Leave my parents out of this,' she demanded angrily. 'Is it beyond your comprehension to understand that I simply don't *want* to go to bed with you?'

'When you respond to me the way you do—yes.'

She knew him well enough to realise the folly of challenging him, but was still unprepared for the speed of his actions as he jerked her against his chest. One hand slid to her nape, his fingers tangling in her curls as he lowered his head and found her mouth with unerring accuracy. His kiss was brief and hard, stinging her lips and leaving her wanting more, but as she melted into him he pulled back and stared down at her, making no attempt to hide his derision.

'I know exactly what you want, Kezia, but I can't force you to be honest with yourself. And one other thing,' he added, as he released her and it became obvious that his scathing comments had rendered her speechless. 'I don't remember asking you to be my mistress. Perhaps you should wait until you're invited before you rush to turn me down.'

His exit line left her seething, and as she prepared for bed she came up with a dozen clever retorts that she could have flung at him if only she'd had her wits about her.

Her anger kept her awake until the early hours as she tossed restlessly beneath the sheets. It didn't help that her body still throbbed with un-fulfilled longing for his possession. She'd never suffered sexual frustration before, or such a desperate, clawing hunger that obliterated common sense and made her behave like a wanton creature in Nik's arms.

If nothing else, it was proof that marriage to Charlie Pemberton would have been disastrous, she acknowledged ruefully. He had been her first lover, but their relationship had been a gentle romance and he had never aroused in her one tenth of the fiery passion she felt for Nik.

With a sigh she sat up and thumped her pillows, needing to expend some of her pent-up physical energy. She wasn't looking for love, she reminded herself as she rolled onto her side, away from the digital clock that flashed three a.m. on the screen. But did she possess the nerve to take her desire for Nik to its logical conclusion? And could she trust herself to remain emotionally uninvolved?

CHAPTER SIX

NIK HAD CALLED the *Atlanta* the pride of the Niarchou fleet, and the description was certainly justified Kezia thought as she glanced around her stateroom. The ship was spectacular, offering luxurious accommodation for three thousand passengers. The brochure she'd found in her room detailed the four swimming pools, dining rooms and show lounges. There was even a gymnasium and golf course.

It was astounding to think that Nik owned this ship, along with her three sister vessels and numerous hotels around the world. The Niarchou Leisure Group had originated from humble beginnings three generations before, and although it had grown to become a global company it was still very much a family business, with Nik at the helm.

Curiously, she had never thought of Nik in

terms of his wealth before. It was the man who intrigued her, not his money. Now, for the first time, she realised the true extent of the Niarchou fortune and her heart sank. They came from different worlds, she acknowledged bleakly, and she had no place in his life.

Slowly she wandered through from her room into the adjoining sitting room, with its wide sweep of windows that overlooked a private balcony. An interconnecting door on the opposite wall led to Nik's stateroom, but the door was closed and she'd learned from the cabin maid, Maria, that Mr Niarchou had not yet arrived on board.

He was cutting it fine, Kezia thought concernedly. The ship was due to leave Southampton dock in less than an hour, and her heart fluttered at the prospect of seeing him again. They had spoken on the phone a few times during the week, but their conversations had been brief and strictly about work issues.

From the coolness of his tone she'd gathered that he was still furious with her, and she hadn't found the courage to enquire about his father. For all kinds of reasons it would be better if their relationship reverted to that of employer and staff. Common sense dictated that she should take no more than a polite interest in his private life, but she couldn't forget the shadows in his eyes when he'd revealed his concern for his father. She cared about him more than she should, she conceded heavily. But for her own good it was imperative that she harden her heart against him.

A tap on the door made a mockery of that resolve, and her pulse-rate accelerated as she crossed the room—only to plummet once more when she discovered Maria in the corridor.

'Mr Niarchou has sent a message to say he regrets that he is unable to join the ship today,' the friendly maid explained. 'He has been unavoidably detained, but will meet you in Lisbon in two days' time.'

'I see. Thank you, Maria.' Kezia forced a smile that disguised her disappointment. Two more days seemed like a lifetime, and it was frightening to acknowledge how much she longed to see him again. So much for hardening her heart, she thought dismally. Where Nik was concerned hers had the consistency of a marshmallow.

'He also requested that I give you these,' Maria

added, as she presented Kezia with an enormous bouquet of roses. 'Enjoy your trip.'

The blooms were exquisite, with their tightly furled petals of dark red velvet and a perfume that was innately sensual. Kezia buried her face in them and inhaled the heady fragrance before fumbling to open the attached envelope. The note was brief and to the point, in Nik's inimitable style.

Roses remind me of you—beautiful to look at but prickly to hold. Don't jump ship. Nik.

Her lips twitched, and at the same time her eyes filled with tears. Dear God, how was she going to handle three weeks at sea with him? And how could she ever contemplate a life without him?

Two days later her stateroom was filled with the scent of roses, providing a powerful reminder of the man who had sent them. Not that she needed reminding of him, Kezia thought as she changed for dinner. She'd spent the whole day in a state of nervous tension, expecting him to arrive on the ship at any moment, but now, as evening fell, there was still no sign of him.

The *Atlanta* had left behind the grey shores of England and was now in the Atlantic Ocean, having stopped first at Vigo, on the coast of Portugal, and now at Lisbon, where Nik had said he would join her. Tomorrow the ship would head for Gibraltar, where the itinerary promised an excursion ashore to explore the great rock. But she was more concerned with Nik's whereabouts than riding the cable car to visit the famous apes.

With a sigh of frustration she opened her wardrobe and selected one of her new evening dresses—a floor-length sea-green sheath with narrow shoulder straps and a daringly low-cut bodice. It had seriously dented her bank balance, but she'd refused point-blank to charge it to the credit card Nik had given her.

The dress was worth every penny, she decided as she studied the graceful folds of the skirt in the mirror. She had left her hair loose, so that it fell halfway down her back in a mass of curls, making her look softer and undeniably sexy she noted with a groan. Much as she wanted to deny it, she had chosen the dress with Nik in mind.

She'd wanted to please him, to catch the flare of desire in his gaze when he looked at her, But Nik wasn't here, and she faced going to dinner alone.

She was seriously tempted to forgo her place at the Captain's table in favour of cabin service, but reminded herself that as Nik's PA it was her duty to represent him in his absence. After completing her make-up, she applied perfume to her pulse-points, snatched up her purse and opened the door to the sitting room—only to stop dead in her tracks as a familiar figure swung round from the window.

'Nik! I had no idea… When did you arrive?'

'An hour or so ago. But I went straight to meet the Captain,' he replied smoothly, his lashes falling to hide the flare of pleasure her appearance had evoked.

He strolled over to the bar, lifted a bottle of champagne from the ice bucket and filled two glasses. She was not as self-assured as she would like him to believe, he noted, catching the faint tremor of her hand as she reached to take the glass he offered. He felt a surge of satisfaction at the evidence that he still disturbed her. She had been in his thoughts constantly this last week, but nothing compared with seeing her in the flesh. And what exquisite flesh, he mused, feeling his body stir. The soft folds of her dress clung to her curves and moulded her breasts, offering them up like ripe peaches that begged for his attention. For a moment he envisaged sliding the diamanté shoulder straps down her arms, so that the creamy globes spilled into his hands, imagined lowering his head and taking first one and then the other dusky pink nipple into his mouth and hearing her soft cries of pleasure as he suckled her.

Enough, he ordered himself firmly, moving away from her while he sought to bring his raging hormones under control. He had made the mistake of rushing her before, and was determined not to do so again. Kezia was a volatile mix of emotions and she needed careful handling. He knew from the soft flush of colour on her cheeks and the tremulous curve of her mouth that she was not immune to him, but for some reason she was fighting her own private battle, and he would have to pursue her with a degree of patience that did not come easily to him.

'How is your father?' she queried huskily.

'Weak, but determined not to show it. He has indomitable will-power,' Nik told her proudly, his voice filled with affection for the man he respected above all others.

'I wondered where you'd got it from,' Kezia murmured dryly, her heart kicking in her chest as he stepped closer. 'I'm glad he's okay; staying in hospital isn't much fun…I guess,' she added awkwardly, aware of the sudden curiosity in glance.

She wasn't about to detail the year she'd spent battling not just leukaemia, but also the effects of the treatment. There was no reason to tell him of the illness that had nearly cost her her life, or of its devastating legacy. She was unaware of the sudden shadows in her eyes as he slid his hand beneath her chin and gently tilted her face to his.

'Don't look so sad, *pedhaki mou*. My father's a fighter, and he isn't ready to give up yet. You have an unexpectedly soft heart,' he murmured, as he noted the glimmer of tears in her eyes.

She swallowed at the latent warmth of his gaze. 'Beneath my prickly exterior, you mean?' Her mouth curved into a smile as she remembered his note. 'Thank you for the roses. They're beautiful.'

'My pleasure.'

He towered over her, heart-stoppingly handsome in his black dinner suit and snowy white shirt. His eyes were dark enough to drown in, and, trapped in his gaze, she swayed towards him, forgetting everything but the need to feel his mouth on hers. She couldn't think straight when he was near, and all her carefully constructed barriers tumbled as she breathed in the exotic musk of his aftershave. He must have come straight from the shower. The hair at his nape was still damp, and she longed to slide her fingers into it, guide his head down to hers and lose herself in the glory of his kiss. Uttering a soft sigh, she parted her lips in unwitting invitation.

'I understand Captain Panos has invited us to join him for dinner? It wouldn't do to be late,' Nik murmured gently, and broke the fierce sexual tension that shimmered between them.

Kezia inhaled sharply and instantly stepped away from him, her face burning. As rejections went, it had been sensitively done—but she still felt as though he had slapped her. What had she expected? she thought miserably as she followed him along the rabbit warren of narrow corridors to the dining room. He was probably sick to death of her blowing hot and cold, and it was entirely her fault that she had no control over her emotions where he was concerned.

Captain Panos was a Greek sailor of thirty years' experience—fifteen of which he had spent working aboard Niarchou cruise liners. He stood as they approached the top table, and greeted Nik as if he was his long-lost son before turning to Kezia.

'Miss Trevellyn—I'm delighted to have the pleasure of your company once again. It's good that your escort has finally shown up, hmm?' he joked in his heavily accented English. 'I'm surprised at you, Nik, for leaving this beautiful young lady alone for even one day. It's not like you to be so careless, my friend,' he added, his eyes gleaming with humour.

'It's a situation I intend to remedy for the rest of the trip,' Nik murmured, the warmth of his gaze causing Kezia to blush self-consciously as she slid into her seat.

She had met several of the guests who were seated around the table the previous evening— notably the brash American billionaire Des Norris.

'So you're Nikos Niarchou?' Des said loudly,

extending a podgy hand towards Nik. 'Damn fine ship you've got here, sir. And that's quite a compliment coming from me. I demand the best for my money—don't I, Marlene? This is my wife Marlene,' he continued, without giving the woman at his side time to speak, 'and my daughter Sammy-Jo.'

Des introduced a strikingly pretty girl whose face seemed to be set in a permanently bored expression. At the sight of Nik the young girl's eyes lit up, and she directed her smile at him whilst managing to completely ignore Kezia.

'Hi—it's great to meet you, Nik. You don't mind if I call you Nik do you?'

She shook her platinum blonde hair over her shoulder in a plainly provocative gesture that Kezia found irritating. She guessed the girl to be no more than seventeen or eighteen, but youth obviously presented no handicap for Sammy-Jo. She was openly flirting with Nik—who didn't appear too troubled by the attention Kezia noted dourly. Of course with his looks and charisma, not to mention a handy multimillion-pound fortune, he was bound to be the most sought-after catch on the trip. The fact was unlikely to have escaped him, but he didn't have to look as though he was enjoying the American girl's eager advances quite so much, she thought, as she forced herself to take a forkful of a seafood cocktail that suddenly tasted as interesting as sawdust.

'You're very quiet. Is something wrong?' Nik murmured towards the end of the meal, when she was trying to summon up enthusiasm for her *crème brulée.*

The cuisine was out of this world, with sumptuous menus offering an extensive choice of superbly prepared dishes. Kezia had been panicking as she'd envisaged piling on the pounds, and had even contemplated trying out one of the aerobics classes, but it seemed that jealousy was an excellent appetite suppressant.

'I'm fine. What could possibly be wrong?' she replied coolly. 'The food is wonderful.'

'But you don't view the company with quite such enthusiasm?' he guessed, his eyes gleaming with amusement as he studied her frown. 'Despite her couture gown, and the rather blinding array of diamonds at her throat, I imagine Sammy-Jo is younger than she looks, and I have no interest in spoilt little girls.'

'It's really none of my business.' Kezia tore her gaze from his and smiled politely at Des Norris as he addressed her in the booming voice that drew the attention of everyone at the table.

'So, what made you decide to come on this cruise, Kezia?' he demanded as he leaned across the table and leered at her cleavage. 'An attractive, single young woman travelling alone— maybe you're hoping for a little on-board romance, eh?'

'Actually, I'm Mr Niarchou's personal assistant. And romance is the last thing on my agenda,' she replied sweetly, refusing to glance at Nik, although she was aware of his soft chuckle.

Sammy-Jo was patently delighted. 'I thought you two were an item. But I guess there's no reason why you can't dance with me, Nik.' She grinned unrepentantly as she tugged him to his feet and flicked an uninterested glance at Kezia. 'You don't mind, do you?'

'Be my guest.' Kezia knew Nik was far too much of a gentleman to publicly embarrass Sammy-Jo by refusing to dance with her, but she couldn't control the sick feeling in the pit of her stomach as the young girl dragged him onto the dance floor and slotted into his arms as if she belonged there.

Murmuring her excuses to the remaining guests seated at the table, she headed purposefully towards the doors leading out onto the deck. Perhaps a dose of fresh air would cool her temper? she thought as she drew her stole around her shoulders and stared out across the moonlit sea. From the admiring glances Nik had received as he'd walked onto the dance floor, she guessed he would have no shortage of willing partners—not least the excitable Sammy-Jo. She didn't care *who* he danced with, Kezia reminded herself fiercely. She was his secretary, nothing more.

With a heavy sigh she began to wander back across the deck, intent on returning to her cabin, when a familiar figure from the past stepped out of the shadows.

'Hello, Kezia.'

'Charlie!' For a few seconds she was almost speechless with shock. 'What are *you* doing here?'

'Working, believe it or not.' Charles Pemberton's face broke into a wide grin as he strolled towards her. 'I run my own travel agency business—catering for the top end of the holiday market, of course,' he added unashamedly.

'I wouldn't have expected anything else,' Kezia replied, her lips twitching. Charlie possessed an easy charm, and his good humour was hard to resist.

'I'm here to report on the *Atlanta*'s new refit. I like to give my clients a first hand account of the trips I'm trying to sell them. And the Niarchou Group has really surpassed itself this time; the facilities on board the ship are superb,' he said admiringly. 'But enough of me. What about you, Kezia? I noticed your name on the passenger list, and I was determined to find you, but I admit I was surprised to see you at the Captain's table with Nikos Niachou tonight. Don't tell me you're his latest flame?' he joked, unable to disguise his curiosity.

'Certainly not. I'm his PA, and this is a working trip for me too.'

'In that case I can safely offer to buy you a drink without fear of reprisal from a six-foot-plus Greek,' Charlie said with a satisfied smile.

Kezia hesitated; Charlie represented the past, and although he no longer had the power to affect her she still viewed the ending of their engagement with sadness. 'I'm not sure…sometimes Nik likes to work late.'

'He looked pretty cosy with the energetic blonde from your table when I walked past the dance floor,' Charlie assured her cheerfully. 'He can't make demands on every minute of your time, surely?'

No, but he filled her mind exclusively every waking minute, Kezia acknowledged silently. Her fascination with Nik was bordering on the obsessive and for the sake of her sanity it had to stop.

'I'd love to have a drink with you, Charlie,' she said firmly. 'We've a lot of catching up to do.'

Forcing a bright smile, she followed the young Englishman into the bar, where a pianist was playing a medley of popular tunes.

'I understand you're a married man now?' she murmured as Charlie assisted her onto a tall bar stool. The cocktail he had ordered her tasted deliciously fruity, but she detected the kick of vodka and sipped it cautiously. 'I saw a photo of you and Amanda in the newspaper.' His marriage to Amanda Heatherington, daughter of a peer, had gained extensive coverage in the British press.

Charlie looked embarrassed. 'Yes, the parents were pleased. They've been friends with Amanda's family for years—' He broke off, his face suddenly serious. 'I'm sorry things didn't work out for us, Kezia. We had some good times together, didn't we?'

'Yes, we did,' Kezia agreed gently. 'But I think we always knew we weren't right for each other, and your family were never happy about us—especially when they found out that I'm unable to have children. I'm glad you're with Amanda,' she told him honestly. 'But I can't believe you didn't bring her on the cruise with you.'

'I'm only going as far as Rome, and then I'm flying home. Amanda didn't want to travel with the baby…' He paused uncertainly before admitting, 'We have a three-month-old son.'

'Charlie, that's fantastic!' Kezia was genuinely pleased.

'Yeah, he's the greatest,' he grinned, unable to hide his paternal pride. 'I've got some photos…but maybe you'd rather not see them.' His cheeks reddened and he dropped his gaze, aware that it was a sensitive issue for her.

'I'd love to see them,' she reassured him softly.

Charlie's frown cleared and he pulled several pictures out of his wallet and handed them to her. The sight of the tiny face peeping from the folds of a shawl hurt more than she had expected, and Kezia felt a sharp pang in her chest. She dealt with it, and smiled, her eyes clear as she glanced up at him. 'He's beautiful; congratulations.'

She took a long sip of her drink, suddenly grateful for the heady feeling it induced. The tears that burned her eyelids were an unwelcome surprise. There was no point in crying. It wouldn't change anything and would probably embarrass Charlie. She was pleased for him—especially when she remembered the pressure he'd been under from his family to produce an heir.

She drained her glass, and had gathered up her purse, ready to return to her cabin, when a deep, husky voice sounded from behind her, sending a quiver the length of her spine.

'So this is where you're hiding. I've been looking for you,' Nik murmured silkily, although she was aware of the note of censure in his voice. 'Won't you introduce me to your friend, *pedhaki mou?*'

He had used the endearment deliberately, Kezia was sure, and she stiffened as his hand settled heavily on her shoulder in a blatantly pro-prietorial gesture. 'This is Mr Pemberton. We were at university together,' she explained stiffly. 'And this is Nikos Niarchou.'

'Nice to meet you, Mr Niarchou,' Charlie said a shade nervously as Nik surveyed him with a cool, hard stare. 'Fantastic ship. I'll certainly be recommending it through my agency.'

'I'm glad to hear it,' Nik drawled. 'Goodnight, Mr Pemberton.'

'Right—well, I'll be off, then. Maybe we can meet up tomorrow for a game of tennis, Kezia?' He kissed her awkwardly on the cheek, and dis-appeared with rather more haste than dignity.

'Do you mind?' Kezia turned on Nik as soon as Charlie was out of earshot. 'He's an old friend, and you were incredibly rude.'

'You can hardly lecture *me* on manners when you left our table without a word,' he retorted, unfazed by the storm brewing in her eyes. 'I've been scouring the ship for you.'

'There was no need; I'm perfectly capable of looking after myself. I couldn't tell you I was leaving because you had your hands full—literally—with Sammy-Jo,' she added coldly.

'And now I'm here, to escort you back to your cabin. Do you have any idea how much attention you're attracting in that dress?' he demanded harshly. 'Your *friend*'s eyes were on stalks.'

With her lush curves exposed by the dipping neckline of her dress, and her silky curls tumbling over her bare shoulders, she could have been one of the legendary sirens who lured men to their death on the rocks. She was a temptation that was testing his will-power to the limit, and he would be damned if he would sit back and allow some floppy-haired Englishman to drool over her, Nik vowed savagely.

'Rubbish,' Kezia snapped, stung by his tone. 'Anyway, I'm not ready to go back yet. I'd like another drink.' She had the beginnings of a headache, and wanted nothing more than to seek the peace and quiet of her cabin, but some imp of mischief in her head was intent on challenging Nik. 'Don't let me keep you,' she murmured sweetly, as she beckoned to the barman.

'You are trying my patience, *pedhaki mou*,' he warned softly. 'I think you've consumed enough alcohol for one night. Particularly as you rarely drink.'

'I feel like living dangerously.' She met his dark gaze and shivered at the unfathomable expression in their depths. She knew she was playing with fire but, hell, she was bored with always taking the safe options in life.

Seeing Charlie and, more importantly, the photos of his baby son had brought home to her how much she had lost. She would never cradle her own child in her arms and the life she had planned—a home filled with children—was a shattered dream that she hadn't completely come to terms with.

Why *shouldn't* she have some fun? she demanded silently as she sipped her cocktail. Life was for living; she knew that better than most. Why not seize whatever Nik was offering, even if it was only a brief fling? What harm could it do?

'So you and Pemberton met at university?' Nik murmured. 'Were you friends, or lovers?'

'We were engaged. Charlie was my fiancé— I've mentioned him before,' Kezia replied steadily. 'But his family made no secret of the fact that they were against the match. For several reasons.' The most pertinent of which she had no intention of revealing.

'Did Pemberton end the engagement?' Nik was studying her intently, as if determined to prise the truth out of her, and she sighed.

'I've told you—ultimately it was a mutual decision, but I understood the pressure he was under. His family hoped he would marry someone with suitably blue blood, and now he has,' she added, unaware of the shadows in her eyes as she met Nik's gaze. She took another sip of her drink, grimacing slightly at the cloying sweetness of pineapple and mango juice which masked the taste of spirits. The second drink hadn't been a good idea, she conceded as the room swayed alarmingly.

'I think you've had enough of that,' Nik drawled in a faintly amused tone that inflamed her temper. She drained the glass and glared at him belligerently.

'You're not my keeper,' she told him crossly.

'No, I'm your incredibly patient boss, who's just about to escort you to your cabin—if I don't have to carry you,' he added dulcetly.

Kezia would have liked to march out of the bar without giving him a backward glance, but instead found herself grateful for his supporting

arm around her waist. The deck seemed to be
slanted at a peculiar angle, and the blast of fresh
air made her head spin.

'I warned you I get seasick,' she told him
when they finally reached their suite. He
glanced at her, not bothering to conceal his impatience. 'If you feel ill, it's entirely self-
induced, so don't look to me for sympathy.
Can you manage to get into bed, or do you
need my help?'

There was no polite answer to that, and she
stormed over to her room in dignified silence
that was ruined when she caught her heel in the
hem of her dress and tripped.

'*Theos!* You would drive a saint to distraction,' he muttered as he caught her and swung
her into his arms.

The sudden contact with the hard wall of his
chest was too much for her senses to cope with.
She could feel the warmth of his skin emanating
through his fine silk shirt, and glimpsed dark
chest hair at his throat, where he had unfastened
the top couple of buttons.

'Put me down. I can manage,' she told him as she
wriggled furiously in his grasp. This was danger-

ous territory. Already she could feel her muscles relax as liquid heat coursed through her veins.

'I noticed,' he answered dryly, ignoring her request and carrying her into her cabin, where he deposited her on the bed. 'Let's get shot of those heels. That way you may have some chance of standing upright.'

He dealt with the buckles of her strappy sandals with deft movements but the brush of his hands on her ankles was enough to make her shiver with pent-up need. He was kneeling by the side of the bed, his hair gleaming like polished jet in the lamplight, and she longed to run her fingers through it.

'Nik…' Her soft whisper brought his head up, and she heard him sigh.

'You've had too much to drink, *pedhaki mou*. You'll feel better in the morning.'

'I'm not drunk,' she assured him solemnly. 'I know what I want.'

'And what is that?'

'I want you to kiss me,' she said simply. It was the truth, and there was no point in denying it.

For a second heat blazed in his eyes, before his lashes fell, concealing his emotions. His face was a taut mask, his bone structure so perfect, that she raised her hand and traced the sharp line of his cheekbone with her finger.

'You're so beautiful, Nik.' Saying what was in her heart suddenly seemed so simple, and she watched, transfixed, as his mouth curved into a rueful smile.

'It's debatable who you're going to hate most in the morning. Yourself or me,' he said gently. 'But unfortunately my will-power to resist you is almost non-existent.'

He moved to sit beside her on the bed, his eyes never leaving hers as he tilted her chin and slowly lowered his head. As his mouth fastened on hers she uttered a low murmur of approval and parted her lips, shuddering with pleasure at the first sweep of his tongue. He took it slow and sensual, tasting her with a level of enjoyment that was evident from his low groan as she responded with uninhibited passion.

This was where she was meant to be, she accepted. When she was in Nik's arms she forgot the past and was uncaring of the future. Here and now was all that mattered, and she urged her body closer to his, desperate for him to remove the barrier of their clothes so that she could feel his skin against hers. A tremor of excitement ran through her when she felt him slide the zip of her dress down her spine. She was aware of him easing the straps over her shoulders, but then he stopped, his mouth gentle on hers as he ended the kiss and turned her away from him.

'Here, put this on.' He thrust her lacy nightdress into her hands and she stared at it in confusion.

'But I thought—' She broke off, her eyes the colour of the sea on a stormy day as she swung her head round to stare at him. 'I want you to stay,' she whispered, her heart thudding painfully in her chest as he stepped away from the bed.

He seemed very big and tall, but it was not just his size that overwhelmed her—it was the man himself. His eyes still glittered with desire, but incredibly it seemed that he had decided against taking up her offer. Had she misunderstood the heat in his gaze? Had her eager capitulation aroused his contempt rather than his lust? Scalding colour flooded her cheeks, and she was unaware of the utter misery evident in the droop of her mouth that almost saw him denounce chivalry and pull her into his arms once more.

'I've obviously made a huge mistake,' she said stiffly, wishing that he would stop staring at her with an expression that looked horribly like sympathy. She didn't need him to feel *sorry* for her, damn it!

'No, you're not mistaken about my desire for you, Kezia. But your timing is appalling. When I make love to you it will be because you really want it, not because your judgement is clouded with alcohol,' he told her bluntly, smiling softly, as if to lessen the sting of his rejection. 'I fear I have too much pride to make a good consolation prize,' he added quietly.

'You're not. A consolation prize for *what?*' she demanded through an agony of embarrassment.

'For your English lover, Charles Pemberton. I saw the sadness in your eyes tonight, *pedhaki mou,* the regrets for what might have been. But your fiancé chose to marry another woman, and until you can come to terms with the past I can't see that we have a future. Try to sleep now,' he bade her, when she sat unmoving on the bed, clutching her nightgown to her chest as if it was a life raft.

He wondered if she had any idea how vulnerable she looked, with the shimmer of tears making her stunning eyes seem too big for her pale face. Not just vulnerable but innately sensual, he admitted grimly as he stepped out of her cabin and closed the door. His body throbbed uncomfortably with unfulfilled desire, but he refused to take advantage of her in her alcohol-induced, highly emotive state. With a muttered oath he poured himself a large brandy before heading for the shower.

CHAPTER SEVEN

MORNING BROUGHT GLORIOUS sunshine streaming into Kezia's cabin. For a few seconds after
she woke she lay still, watching the sunbeams
dancing on the ceiling, but almost instantly her
memory returned, and she groaned as she buried
her head beneath her pillow. Perhaps the events
of the previous evening had been a bad dream?
she wondered. But she knew it was the faint hope
of a drowning man—or in this case woman.

The sight of her dress, lying in a pool of green
silk on the floor where she had dropped it, was
evidence, if any were necessary, that last night's
fiasco had taken place. Her gaze settled on her
sandals, neatly stacked beneath a chair, and a
shudder went through her as she remembered
the feel of Nik's hands on her ankles as he'd
eased the shoes from her feet.

What had she done? The answer was almost too unbearable to contemplate. She had made an utter fool of herself. And although it was tempting to blame her behaviour on the exotic cocktails, she accepted with searing honesty that she had been fully aware of her actions. She had made a play for Nik, had practically begged him to kiss her, and when he had done so she had responded with such wild abandon that he had been left in no doubt that she wanted him to take her to bed.

So why hadn't he? she wondered painfully. His rejection had been gentle, and he'd spouted some nonsense about her still having feelings for Charlie, but it had been a rejection nonetheless, and she didn't think she could ever face him again. The plain truth was that he didn't want her, she acknowledged miserably. She'd probably embarrassed him, and had certainly embarrassed herself but even if she handed in her resignation immediately she would still have to work a month's notice—three weeks of which would be spent trapped here on the *Atlanta* with him.

The ship had to be the most luxurious prison in the world, she though wryly as she headed for the shower. But right now she would give anything to escape back to her flat, where she could bask in Max's devotion and kid herself that she had never even heard of a man called Nikos Niarchou.

He rapped on her door while she was combing her wet hair and she stiffened, every muscle in her body clenched in fear that he would walk in.

'Rise and shine—it's almost nine o'clock,' he called through the closed door. 'There's a mass of work to catch up on today.'

He sounded his usual whirlwind self, and for once she was glad of his impatience. She dressed swiftly in a simple navy skirt and white blouse, swept her hair into a businesslike knot on top of her head, and took a deep breath before going out to meet him.

'I ordered the continental breakfast,' he said, barely lifting his head from his laptop as she joined him at the table. 'The coffee's hot, help yourself.'

He had opened the patio door, so that a warm sea breeze lightly tugged the corner of the table-cloth. The ocean was an intense blue, the sky a shade lighter, dotted with tiny wisps of cotton wool clouds, and Kezia inhaled the fresh air as she slid into her seat. Only then did he look up, and she felt herself blush as she met his speculative gaze.

'Sleep well?'

'Yes, thank you.'

It was a blatant lie, and Nik studied the bruises beneath her eyes for several minutes before returning his attention to his computer screen.

She looked as fragile as fine porcelain this morning, the tremor of her hand as she poured herself a cup of coffee evidence that she was not as self-assured as her neat appearance suggested. He wondered what she would do if he strode round the table, swept her into his arms and kissed her with all the pent-up frustration that had kept him awake until the early hours. She would probably throw the coffee at his head he acknowledged wryly, and forced himself to concentrate on the complicated report in front of him.

The next few hours were devoted entirely to work. Kezia was grateful to be back on familiar territory, where conversation with Nik related only to business, and gradually she relaxed to the point where she no longer felt as though she wanted to die of embarrassment whenever she caught his gaze.

When she eventually took a break she was surprised to find that it was past lunchtime, and she left him deeply involved in a conference call while she stepped out onto the private balcony. The ship was sailing down the Spanish coast to Gibraltar, and all around the huge expanse of sea sparkled in the brilliant sunshine. It was a far cry from the cold air and gloomy skies of England, she thought as she lifted her face to the sun. Working for Nik was a dream job, if only she could control her feelings for him.

'How do you fancy pizza for lunch?'

He suddenly materialised at her side, looking urbane and utterly gorgeous in beige chinos and a black polo shirt, his eyes shaded by designer sunglasses. She felt the tenuous hold on her control instantly crumble, and tore her eyes from him to stare at the horizon.

'There's a pizzeria overlooking the pool, if you'd like to eat outside.'

'Sounds good.' She managed just the right amount of cool enthusiasm in her voice as she awarded him a brief smile.

'Do I detect a thaw in the big freeze?' he queried, the gentle amusement in his voice bringing her head round.

'What did you expect?' she muttered awkwardly. 'I made a complete fool of myself last night.'

'Don't be so hard on yourself, *pedhaki mou*. Everyone drinks more than they should at least once in their lifetime.'

Innate honesty made her confess, 'I wasn't drunk. I knew what I was doing.'

He had moved closer without her being aware of it, and she turned to find him caging her against the railings, his muscular brown arms forming a barrier on either side of her. 'I'm glad to hear it,' he murmured softly, seconds before his head blotted out the sunlight.

His lips claimed hers in an evocative caress that broke through her reserve. Her senses flared as she inhaled the clean, seductive scent of him, and she lost the will to resist him as his tongue explored the contours of her lips before dipping between them to initiate an intimate exploration. She was losing her grip on reality as she slid into a place dominated by sensation, but even as her arms crept up around his neck her brain was urgently reminding her that she could not bear another rejection. Somehow she found the strength to break the kiss, and stared up at him in confusion.

'But I thought… You don't want…'

'Of course I want you, Kezia. I don't think my hunger for you can be in any doubt, do you?' he added, his voice suddenly harsh as he relaxed the savage control he'd imposed on his muscles and leaned into her.

The rigid proof of his arousal pushing against her belly should have shocked her, but instead she was filled with a mixture of tenderness and fierce exultation. He was not as in control as he would like her to believe and the knowledge gave her a heady feeling of feminine power.

'Then why did you walk away last night?' she whispered. 'I've spent the past twelve hours despising myself for my weakness where you're concerned,' she added indignantly, her temper triggered by the memory of the hours of mental torture she had suffered.

She frowned as she recalled his words from the previous night, when he'd told her there was no future for them while she still cared for Charlie.

She'd never envisaged a future with Nik that lasted longer than a couple of months anyway, she thought bleakly, unaware that he could read the emotions that chased across her face.

'My engagement to Charlie ended two years ago. I'm not in love with him. We're friends, that's all.'

'Then why did you look so sad last night?' Nik demanded fiercely. 'Do you think I didn't notice the longing in your eyes when you looked at him? I notice everything about you,' he muttered, seeming as taken aback as she was by this last statement.

'It wasn't because of Charlie. I was just re-membering the good times we'd had at univer-sity—' She broke off helplessly, unable to reveal the real reason for the ache in her heart. 'Life seemed simpler then,' she admitted quietly.

Seeing the pictures of Charlie's baby son had evoked a powerful maternal instinct within her that would never be fulfilled. Last night the future had beckoned, lonely and loveless. It was little wonder that she had wanted to lose herself in the passion Nik's burning gaze seemed to promise.

'I'm not in love with him,' she insisted, her

heart flipping in her chest at the sudden warmth of Nik's smile.

'Then I'll try to restrain myself from rearranging Mr Pemberton's features when I next see him,' Nik murmured lightly. 'I'm starving. Let's go and find that pizza.'

Kezia stretched out on her sunbed and wriggled her shoulders blissfully. The beach at Nice in the South of France was busy, but not unpleasantly so. The sand was dotted with brightly coloured parasols and the air rang with the sound of children's laughter and the gentle lap of the waves on the shore. It wasn't a bad way to make a living, she thought wryly as she stared up at the azure blue sky. She couldn't help but feel a fraud—especially when she remembered her various friends who were toiling away in London office blocks.

To be fair, she had done *some* work during the past week, while the *Atlanta* had cruised the Mediterranean, stopping at Valencia, Barcelona and Marseille, before arriving at the bustling resort of Nice. Each morning she joined Nik on their private patio for breakfast before settling down to several hours at her laptop whilst he ran his global empire from the ship. But after lunch they invariably relaxed around the pool—or, if the ship was in port, went ashore to explore the sights.

It was a lifestyle she could easily grow accustomed to, Kezia decided as she rolled onto her stomach and peeped at the man stretched out beside her. Nik in swimming shorts was a sight to behold, and she felt the familiar squirmy feeling in the pit of her stomach as her eyes travelled over his broad chest, with its covering of dark hairs, his flat stomach and strong thighs. At that point her gaze skidded to a halt, and she hastily buried her head in her arms. The molten heat that surged through her had nothing to do with the warmth of the sun, and she sighed as she felt her breasts swell and tighten.

'Are you too hot, *pedhaki mou?*' Nik's deep-timbred tones sent a quiver through her.

Oh, my—how was she to answer that? She was burning up.

'Your skin is so fair, you must take care not to burn,' he said seriously as he rolled onto one hip and studied her flushed face. 'Shall I put some more sun cream on your back?'

'No! I'm fine,' she replied quickly. No way could she cope with his hands sliding over her body, smoothing oil onto her skin with frankly sensuous movements. It had been purgatory when she'd agreed to it an hour ago and her hormones were in such a stew she would probably self-combust.

'It's no trouble,' he assured her gravely.

She was sure the devil was laughing at her, but his eyes were hidden behind his shades and as usual his thoughts were a mystery to her. This past week had seen a new era in their relationship. She could no longer kid herself that he was simply her boss now that he took advantage of every opportunity to kiss her. Not that she was complaining, she acknowledged, her nerve endings tingling as she remembered the touch of his mouth on hers, the evocative caresses that hinted at his barely leashed passion. When Nik turned on the charm he was impossible to resist. She had revelled in his attention as they discussed every topic under the sun and yet carefully steered clear of the subject of the fierce sexual awareness that simmered between them like volcanic lava ready to explode.

'I'm going to cool off in the sea,' she told him

as she tore her gaze from his face and jumped to her feet.

Jumping had not been a good move, she conceded silently, as her breasts fought to escape the tiny triangles of emerald Lycra that purported to be a bikini.

On their first trip to the pool Nik had taken one look at her functional black one-piece and hauled her off to the on-board boutiques.

'You can't sit on the beaches of the Côte D'Azur looking like you're a Victorian governess. Most women go topless, you know.'

'I'm not most women,' Kezia had pointed out firmly, as she'd watched him select half a dozen bikinis in rainbow shades.

In the ensuing argument over who would pay for them, which he had eventually won, she hadn't bothered to try them on—something that she deeply regretted now, she decided grimly, as his eyes travelled down to her hips and the equally minuscule bikini pants.

'You have a gorgeous body, Kezia. Why do you insist on covering it up?' he murmured, his indolent tone at variance with his heated gaze as he watched her wrap a sarong tightly round her. 'You should enjoy having such a fabulous figure. I know *I'd* like to enjoy it,' he added dulcetly, his lips twitching as she threw him a scandalised glare.

'I don't want to burn,' she muttered stiffly before running down to the sea.

He was the bitter end, she thought as she dropped her sarong at the water's edge and plunged into the waves. The level of sexual tension between them was white hot. They were both aware of it. And yet he had made no move to take their relationship further. Despite treating her to wonderful romantic dinners at the *Atlanta*'s various restaurants, and dancing in the nightclub, their bodies closely entwined, he seemed curiously reluctant to take her to his bed.

Perhaps he was waiting for a sign from her— a clear indication that she wanted him to make love to her? she brooded as she struck out into deeper water. It was impossible to believe he really thought she harboured feelings for her ex-fiancé, as he had once accused. She had met up with Charlie a couple of times, and enjoyed his easy company, but Nik could not possibly imagine she felt anything deeper for the younger man than friendship.

Incredibly, she had detected definite signs of jealousy from Nik, and the light-hearted tennis match she'd played with Charlie had been followed by a far more hostile battle between the two men. The fifth set had been played with the seriousness of a Wimbledon final beneath the blazing Mediterranean sun, and unsurprisingly, considering Nik's stronger physique and fierce determination, he had emerged the victor.

She knew Nik desired her—his urgent kisses every night were proof of his hunger—so why couldn't she link her arms around his neck when he escorted her to her cabin and suggest that they fulfil their mutual desperation for each other rather than spend another frustrating night apart? She was scared, she acknowledged as she flipped onto her back and floated on the gentle swell. Not of Nik—her every instinct told her he would couple passion with sensitivity and consideration when he made love to her. It was herself she was afraid of. She had once told him she wasn't looking for love, but dared she risk her emotional security for a few weeks, months at most, of physical pleasure and then walk away when it was over with her pride intact?

Her silent reverie was rudely shattered when she felt something tug at her legs, dragging her beneath the surface. Almost instantly she bobbed back up, spluttering and thrashing her arms wildly as she recalled the old movie about a killer shark. The predator swimming next to her bared his white teeth as he grinned at her unrepentantly.

'You look like a mermaid,' Nik told her as he threaded his fingers through the long strands of her hair that were floating on the water.

'Scaly and with a tail, you mean?' she snapped, as she snatched air into her lungs.

His smile deepened, and he caught hold of her around the waist to pull her up against his chest. 'Definitely no tail,' he assured her, after sliding his hands over her hips to make a thorough investigation of her legs. 'Or scales. Your skin is like satin.'

His shoulders gleamed like burnished bronze in the sunlight, the whorls of dark hair on his chest slightly abrasive against her palms as she was forced to cling to him. She was out of her depth in more ways than one, she thought frantically. She'd never met a man like him and would probably never do so again.

The sea's current was causing them to bob up and down, so that his near naked body rubbed sensuously against hers, creating havoc with her hormones. *Live dangerously, just once,* the voice in her head whispered, and with a low murmur of capitulation she slid her fingers into his hair and drew his mouth down to hers to initiate a kiss that stirred his soul.

Nik waited a heartbeat before taking control and deepening the kiss, cupping her nape so that he could angle her head to his satisfaction. What was it about this woman that made him ache to possess her? he wondered. In his thirty-six years he'd had countless lovers, particularly when he'd been younger and driven by his hormones to follow up every flirtatious glance that came his way. In recent years he had become more selective, but he made no denial that he enjoyed women. He had a high sex drive and a low boredom threshold. There had even been occasions when he'd had a mistress on three continents—elegant socialites who understood that their influence over him ended at the bedroom door. He valued his independence, yet in the past few days he'd found himself wondering if he would ever tire of Kezia's smile, or the way her eyes darkened to the colour of the sea when he kissed her.

A rogue wave took them both by surprise as it lifted them up and propelled them inland. Kezia reluctantly broke the kiss, gasping as she was sucked beneath the surface, but Nik tightened his grip and hauled her up.

'Not so much a mermaid as a drowned rat now,' he teased, and she retaliated by splashing him, before tugging out of his arms and racing up the beach, squealing for mercy when he pulled her down in the shallows.

'Nik, this is a family beach,' she reminded him urgently as he lowered his body onto hers, supporting his weight on his elbows. He was tantalisingly close, and she loved the sound of his laughter as he threw back his head.

'So it is, *pedhaki mou.* I guess I'll have to wait until later to take my retribution.'

The gleam in his eyes caused a tremor of excitement to run through her, but instead of shying away she calmly met his gaze. 'I guess you will,' she whispered, and heard him mutter a fierce imprecation beneath his breath as he dropped a brief, hard kiss on her lips before he stood and tugged her to her feet.

'Would you like to eat on board tonight? Or shall we go back to the ship to shower and change and then return to explore the Old Town? I know of a particularly good seafood restaurant.'

'That sounds nice,' Kezia replied. 'But if I carry on eating the way I have been, I'm going to put on weight.'

'You need to regain the pounds you lost when you were ill,' he told her unconcernedly. 'And I love your curves. Like all Greek men, I prefer real, voluptuous women—not some unhealthy-looking stick insect. I love your bottom,' he said, with stark frankness, 'and the fact that your breasts are doing their best to fall out of your bikini.'

'Whose fault is that?' she demanded, her cheeks scarlet as she struggled to hide the offending bosom beneath her sarong. 'You chose it.'

'True, but I've paid the penalty by spending most of the day in the sea, desperately trying to hide my body's reaction to you,' he said, his unabashed confession rendering her speechless for the whole of the journey back to the ship.

* * *

The night sky was studded with stars—like diamonds on a huge velvet pincushion, Kezia thought as she studied the beautiful canopy above her. The bright lights that marked out the coast were growing fainter as the motor launch sped across the bay back to the *Atlanta*, whose outline was clearly defined by colourful twinkling bulbs.

'Are you cold?' Nik's husky tones sounded close to her ear, and she smiled as he draped her stole over her shoulders. The air was cooler now than during the day, but her shiver had been born of excitement, and a sense of feverish anticipation that could no longer be denied.

They had spent a magical evening exploring the Old Town of Nice, with its wonderful architecture and pretty pastel-coloured buildings, before dining in an exclusive restaurant tucked away down one of the narrow side streets. Nik had been charmingly attentive, their conversation easy, but it had been the unspoken words and shared intimate glances as their gazes met across the table that had left Kezia longing to return to the ship.

'I understand there's a disco tonight, out on deck. Would you like to visit for a while, maybe have a drink?' he murmured once they were safely on board the *Atlanta*. 'Or are you tired, *pedhaki mou?*' There was a wealth of subtle suggestion in his query, causing a quiver to run through her as his breath stirred the tendrils of hair at the nape of her neck.

Definitely not tired, she acknowledged silently. She'd never felt more *alive* in her life. Her senses were heightened to such a degree that she was conscious of the salt tang of the sea carried on the breeze, mingling with the evocative scent of Nik's aftershave. Neither did she want a drink. After the events of a week ago she had stuck religiously to iced water, and tonight it was imperative that she keep a clear head. She didn't want there to be any more misunderstandings between them.

'We could watch the dancing for a while, if you like,' she said huskily, her nerve failing her. She was not some inexperienced virgin, for heaven's sake she reminded herself irritably. She was a grown woman who had made the conscious decision to make love with the man who was slowly driving her insane with need. Why couldn't she smile at him, award him one of the flirtatious glances she'd seen other women send his way, and coolly suggest that they return to the suite?

At the bar, her good intentions dissolved, and she sipped the crisp white wine Nik handed her with a grateful sigh as warmth stole through her veins.

'Dance with me?' he asked softly, a mixture of sympathy and gentle amusement in his dark gaze as he recognised the silent battle raging within her.

It was frightening how well he knew her, she brooded as the music changed to a slow ballad and she slipped into his arms. She had the feeling that he could read her mind, but in many ways he remained a stranger to her—and she had no idea what was in his head.

'Relax,' he murmured, his arm tightening around her waist as she stumbled. He threaded his hand through her hair, and with a sigh she sagged against his chest, closing her mind to everything but the music, the moment, and the man who had stolen her heart.

How long they danced together she did not know. She lost all concept of time, content to stand in the circle of his arms as they swayed with the slow tempo, hips and thighs brushing together as mutual arousal built to a level where there could only be one outcome.

'Ready to go?' His lips feathered her lobe before trailing down her throat to the pulse that jerked frantically at its base.

Wordlessly Kezia nodded, unaware of the stark vulnerability in her eyes that made Nik's gut clench. Somehow, without him understanding the how or the when, she had become infinitely precious to him. How had she slipped beneath his guard to the extent that his own desires took second place to his need to do what was right for her? She was a complicated mixture of emotions—fiercely independent and yet acutely sensitive. He would never knowingly hurt her, he vowed as he brushed his lips over hers and felt his body harden at her instant response.

Already he could not envisage a time without her. He would miss the sound of her laughter, her acidic comments when she dared to answer him back—which she frequently did. He had never met a woman like her, and he accepted that he would want her in his life for a long time—months, years, even, he brooded.

The sobering thought saw him escort her back

to the suite in silence, his mind reeling at the possibility that he wanted more than a brief affair with Kezia. Once inside, he strode across to the bar and poured himself a large brandy.

'Can I get you a drink?'

'No, thank you.'

She had followed him into the room and was hovering by the patio doors, seemingly fascinated by the far-off lights that delineated the coast. In her black lace evening dress and high-heeled sandals she looked elegant and sophisticated, but the rigid set of her shoulders, the way she fiddled restively with her purse, spoke volumes about her nervous tension.

Silently cursing himself, Nik swallowed the contents of his glass in one gulp. He had never needed Dutch courage before in his life—but he'd never pursued a woman with such patience before either, he conceded ruefully; usually he had to fight them off. He had always treated his lovers with respect, and he'd certainly received no complaints, but getting it right had never mattered so much before. He wanted the first time he made love to Kezia to be perfect.

Setting down his glass, he strolled towards her, noting the way she stiffened as he approached.

'Are you interested in the stars?' he asked gently, when she remained staring resolutely at the heavens.

'I know nothing about astronomy,' she replied with a faint smile. 'But on a night like this space seems so infinite and so beautiful, don't you think?'

'Exquisite,' he murmured, his gaze fixed on her delicate features as he turned her in his arms. He glimpsed the faint shimmer of tears, the agonising uncertainty in her gaze, and was flooded with tenderness as well as passion. 'Stay with me?' he whispered, before claiming her mouth, his fingers sliding into her hair to cup her nape.

With every other woman he had taken to bed he'd always felt the need to qualify that statement, to specify that the invitation was for the night only, but with Kezia he was certain that one night would not be enough to satiate the hunger he felt for her.

'I want to make love to you,' he told her as he eased the pressure of his kiss and traced the outline of her lips with his tongue. He needed to spell it out, wanted her to be absolutely sure, and he felt his heart kick painfully in his chest when she nodded wordlessly before she wrapped her arms around his neck and clung tightly, as if she would never let go.

CHAPTER EIGHT

NIK'S STATEROOM WAS slightly bigger than Kezia's, but equally sumptuously appointed, with soft blue velvet carpet, discreet lighting, and a double bed that was the immediate focus of her attention.

She was not here to admire the décor, she thought, her heart pounding as he entwined his fingers through hers and led her through the door. It would have been easier if he had lifted her into his arms and carried her, she acknowledged as her steps slowed. At least then she could convince herself that she had been swept away on a tide of passion. Instead, the decision of whether to stay, or flee to her own cabin, was entirely in her hands.

Was he aware of her apprehension, mixed with an undeniable sense of anticipation? She shivered, and felt every nerve-ending prickle unbearably in a sensation that was closer to pain than pleasure.

'Are you afraid of me, *pedhaki mou?*'

The tenderness inherent in his tone touched a nerve, but she shook her head fiercely. 'Of course not.' She was not afraid of him. But his expectations terrified her.

He was used to worldly-wise, sophisticated women, whose level of expertise between the sheets matched his skilful lovemaking. Self-doubt rocked her. She couldn't possibly compete when her only experience of sex was with Charlie. One lover in twenty-four years hardly made her an expert in the art of seduction, she brooded, unaware that he could read the play of emotions in her eyes.

'You have no idea how often I wish I'd followed my first instincts the day we met in the London office,' he said suddenly, his voice breaking the tense silence. At her look of puzzlement he elaborated. 'I took one look at you and was overwhelmed by the urge to fling you down on your desk, remove your clothes and lose myself inside you—take us both to the heights of sexual ecstasy,' he added steadily when she gaped at him.

'You felt like that *then?*' she whispered incredulously, casting her mind back all those months.

All the days and weeks that she had been beating herself up over her inappropriate feelings for him, and *he* had been feeling them too! Her nervousness dissolved in a flash, aided by the unconcealed hunger in his gaze. Nik wanted her, had always wanted her, and the chemistry she'd felt between them that day had been real, not some figment of her imagination or wishful thinking.

'So what stopped you?' she queried lightly as she laid her palms flat against his chest and felt the erratic thud of his heart beneath her fingertips.

'It would have broken every rule of political correctness and possibly landed me in court on charges of sexual harassment,' he replied with a smile, as his arms came round her to pull her close, so that she was made achingly aware of the power of his arousal. 'And you were not ready, *agape mou.*'

She acknowledged the truth of that with a soft smile, her eyes wide and clear as she murmured, 'I am now. I want you to make love to me, Nik.' Whatever else she might have said was lost beneath the force of his kiss, that plundered her soul and drove every thought from her mind other than her desperate need for him to love her. His tie was quickly discarded, his jacket flung carelessly to the floor, and she scrabbled with his shirt buttons, parting the material to run her hands over the bunched muscles of his abdomen. His skin was like satin, overlaid with a fine covering of dark hairs that arrowed down and disappeared beneath the waistband of his trousers. As he trailed his lips down her neck and traced the line of her collarbone she fumbled with his zip, her inhibitions blown away with the force of her longing to feel him deep inside her.

'We have plenty of time,' he said softly, his mouth curving into a sensuous smile at her eagerness to undress him.

He dealt with his zip and then hers, sliding it the length of her spine so that he could tug her dress from her shoulders. In a black lace bra and matching briefs she was unutterably beautiful, and he inhaled sharply as he reached behind to unfasten the clip so that her bounteous breasts spilled into his hands. He couldn't repress a groan as he took the weight of them in his hands, firm yet deliciously soft.

He shaped their rounded fullness before lowering his head to take one nipple into his mouth.

Kezia whimpered as sensation pierced her. It was exquisite, and she slid her hands into his hair to hold him to his task. His hands roamed her body, cupped her bottom and pulled her hard against his thighs while he transferred his mouth to her other nipple and metred out the same punishment, until she writhed in his arms and cried out, begging him never to stop.

With a low groan he lifted her up, deftly pulled back the bedspread and laid her on sheets that felt blessedly cool on her heated skin. She felt boneless, her limbs heavy and languid, as she opened slumberous eyes to watch him strip down to his boxers. In the lamplight his skin gleamed like copper, and she held her breath as with one swift movement his underwear joined his trousers on the floor and he stood, legs slightly apart, gloriously and unashamedly naked. The full strength of his arousal brought a moment's panic, and she caught her bottom lip with her teeth as she viewed him, imagined him driving into her with firm, hard thrusts. Liquid heat pooled between her thighs, and her fear disappeared as she caught the gentle emotion in his eyes.

'There's no rush, *pedhaki mou*. I want this to be good for you,' he told her as he joined her on the bed and drew her into his arms.

Being held against the warmth of his broad chest was akin to reaching heaven, Kezia thought with a sigh as she burrowed closer. The scent of his cologne mixed with the more subtle drift of male pheromones stirred her senses, and with great daring she nipped one flat nipple with her teeth.

'You know I'll have to repay that in kind,' he teased, as he rolled her flat on her back and took her mouth in a fierce kiss, his tongue probing between her lips to initiate an intimate exploration that left her trembling. He then proceeded to administer the same attention to each of her breasts, taking first one and then the other fully into his mouth and suckling hard, so that heat unfurled in the pit of her stomach and she twisted her hips restlessly.

Her knickers formed a barrier he deftly removed, and she held her breath when he trailed his hands across her stomach and thighs to rest lightly on the tight red curls at their apex. She arched her hips as his fingers gently eased a path, parted her with infinite care and dipped into her to discover her moist inner heat.

'Nik,' she cried out as he probed deeper, stroking her with one finger and then two, forcing her legs to widen so that he could continue the skilful caress.

It was too much. She could feel the waves of sensation building and twisted frantically on the mattress.

'Please—I want you,' she whispered, sure she would die if she did not feel the full length of him inside her.

For a heart-stopping moment he withdrew, and she tensed, terrified that he had for some reason changed his mind. Perhaps she wasn't doing enough to pleasure him, she thought desperately, but as she reached for him he gave a husky laugh.

'Not this time, my sweet Kezia. Not unless you want this to be over before it's begun.'

At the sound of his voice she opened her eyes, her fear that he was about to reject her fading when she realised the reason for his brief hesitation. Now was not the time to explain that there was no need for him to use protection, she thought painfully. The one thing she could be utterly certain of was that she would never conceive his child.

He mistook the sudden shadows in her eyes and hovered above her, the harsh planes of his face thrown into stark relief as he fought to hold himself back.

'If you've changed your mind, you need to say so in the next ten seconds,' he grated.

She could see the frustration mirrored in his gaze, and with it his absolute respect for her. It was her decision, he wouldn't force her and as she stroked the rigid line of his jaw she felt her heart melt.

'I want you. More than I've ever wanted a man in my life. Make love to me, Nik,' she pleaded, and she drew his head down and kissed him.

He muttered something in Greek as he slid his hands beneath her bottom and angled her hips, moving over her so that his throbbing shaft pushed against her. She clung to his shoulders, her eyes locked with the burning heat of his as she parted her legs and felt him ease forward. He took it slow, penetrating her with infinite care, then drawing back a little to enable her muscles to stretch around him.

'Nik!' She wanted more, and moved her hips so that he thrust forward again, deeper this time, filling her so that every atom of her being was focused on the feel of him as he made them one.

He set a rhythm that was as old as time and she matched him, welcomed each stroke by arching her hips and drawing him ever deeper. It was indescribably good, she acknowledged with the tiny part of her brain capable of thought, but as he increased his pace she lost all grip on reality and gave herself up entirely to sensation. Pleasure began to build, in little ripples at first, that grew stronger and more urgent. She dug her fingers into his back, held on tight as the first waves of her climax sent spasms ripping through her body.

Still he drove into her, with strong, steady strokes that were taking her inexorably higher and higher, until she reached the pinnacle and cried out, her breath coming in harsh sobs as she shuddered with the force of her release. Only then did he falter, his face rigid as he fought for control, but as her muscles contracted around him he groaned and surged into her with one last, powerful thrust, before collapsing on top of her.

She should move, Kezia thought. She should

slip out of Nik's arms, gather up her clothes and make some teasing remark about needing to return to her own cabin to get some sleep. She did none of those things. Her body seemed to be held in a state of lassitude that kept her firmly pinned to the mattress, and she could her feel her eyelids drift closed.

'Sleep, *pedhaki mou,*' Nik's voice was as soft as velvet, and as he brushed his lips over hers she was powerless to prevent her response.

His breath was warm on her neck, stirring the tendrils of hair, and she sighed as he settled her comfortably against his chest. She must not cling, the voice in her head sharply reminded her. She must be cool and composed, as if making love with him had been a brief few moments of pleasure rather than the most earth shattering experience of her life.

'I must go back to my room,' she muttered, finding speech difficult when her face was pressed against his chest.

She felt rather than saw his smile. 'But then I'll have to come and find you when I want to make love to you again,' he murmured huskily, sending a quiver through her as she imagined going through the whole process once more. 'And that could be very soon,' he added, his voice laced with sensual promise. 'Stay here with me, Kezia *mou*. I don't want you to go.'

The thought was sufficiently disturbing to keep him awake until dawn, and it was only after she had stirred in his arms and he had taken her again, with tenderness as well as passion, that he finally slept.

Kezia opened her eyes and winced—previously little-used muscles were making themselves known. Not that she was complaining, she thought with a smile as she turned her head on the pillow and found Nik watching her, the softness of his gaze making her heart leap.

'Good morning, *pedhaki mou,*' he greeted her gently, as he had each of the past four mornings that she had woken in his bed.

Did he ever sleep? she wondered as she lifted her hand and ran her fingers over the dark stubble on his jaw. She always fell asleep in his arms, utterly satiated by the passion they'd shared each night, and no matter what time she woke he was lying quietly beside her, watching her.

'Good morning.' She returned his greeting gravely, her senses flaring as he brushed his lips across her fingertips.

Even that fleeting gesture was enough to stir her body into urgent life, she thought despairingly. She felt her breasts swell and quickly pulled the sheet around her, desperately trying to hide the fact that her nipples had hardened to tight, throbbing peaks. Of course he knew the effect he had on her, and his mouth curved into a slow, sensual smile as he studied her flushed cheeks. It was so unfair, she thought bitterly. One look was all it took to reduce her to a mass of quivering emotions, and the moment he touched her she went up in flames.

For the sake of her pride she needed to take control of the situation and bestow a brief kiss on his cheek before collecting her robe and sauntering into the *en-suite* bathroom. The sudden flare of heat in his eyes trapped her to the bed. He was not wholly unaffected by the sizzling chemistry between them, she noted, her satisfaction increasing when she trailed her other hand over his hip and met the rigid proof of his arousal.

'We really should get up and do some work,'

she murmured, the token protest lost beneath the pressure of his mouth as he initiated a kiss that swiftly dispensed with any idea she might have had of trying to resist him. She was a lost cause, she acknowledged, with a sigh that became a moan of pure pleasure as he tugged the sheet away and shaped her breasts with his hands.

'The only urgent business you need to worry about is pleasuring your master,' he growled playfully, and he took her by surprise and flipped her over so that she was lying on top of him. He gently pushed her so that she was straddling him, in a position that gave him perfect access to her breasts. 'Beautiful,' he muttered, his voice slurred with satisfaction and he stroked her, his dark, tanned hands making an erotic contrast with her milky white skin.

Knowing how easily she burned, she had slathered on the sunscreen and was suddenly glad that she hadn't had the nerve to sunbathe topless. She shook her head so that her red curls tumbled over her shoulders, and felt a thrill of feminine pleasure at the way Nik's eyes narrowed. With his hands cupping her ribcage he drew her forward and took one nipple in his mouth, suckling gently before turning his attention to its twin, his tongue flicking across the sensitive peak until she cried out and ground her hips against him. His penis pushed into her belly, and she felt the flood of warmth between her thighs that indicated her readiness to take him inside her.

She had assumed he would roll her onto her back but instead he lifted her and guided her down onto him, his eyes locked with hers as he watched her look of shock slowly change to pleasure. It was the first time he'd allowed her to take control, but her uncertainty quickly disappeared as instinct took over and she set a pace that had him gritting his teeth as he fought to hold back. It was only when he felt her muscles contract around him and heard her sob his name as the first waves of her orgasm hit that his control snapped. With a groan he rolled her over, crushing her beneath him as he drove in, hard and fast, until he could bear it no more and tumbled them both over the edge.

'What would you like to do today?' he queried lazily as he brushed his lips across hers in a lingering caress before rolling onto the mattress beside her. 'I have a meeting scheduled with

Captain Panos later this morning, but we could meet up for lunch.'

'Don't you have any work for me to be getting on with?' she said seriously. 'I've hardly done a thing for the last few days.'

Since leaving Nice, the *Atlanta* had made a leisurely journey down the coast of Italy. They had stopped for two nights at Pisa, and had travelled inland to spend a glorious day exploring the beautiful city of Florence, birthplace of the Renaissance. The rich culture of the city had been almost too much to take in as they'd visited art galleries to view originals by Rubens, Botticelli and Michaelangelo, and Kezia had quietly determined that she would one day return, to spend more time in the place she had instantly loved.

Yesterday the ship had docked again, and Nik had given her a guided tour of Rome, which boasted some of the most incredible architecture she had ever seen. The cruise on the *Atlanta* was turning out to be the experience of a lifetime in more ways than one, she acknowledged ruefully as she admired Nik's naked form when he stood and strolled towards the bathroom.

'There's nothing vital on the agenda,' he assured her with a smile as he saw her sudden frown. 'You're free to do as you like today, *agape mou.*'

'In that case I might go ashore again and do some shopping. I promised Anna I'd bring her a souvenir from every place we stopped.'

'Good—you can choose some baby clothes while you're there.'

Nik had disappeared into the bathroom and so did not see the look of acute shock on her face. What on earth was he talking about? He had used protection every time they'd made love, and she hadn't yet steeled herself to explain that it was impossible for her to fall pregnant.

'I think it's a bit premature to be worrying about that,' she muttered, her voice sticking in her throat as a wave of desolation swept over her. Even if by some miracle he fell in love with her and begged her to be the mother of his child, she would never cradle Nik's baby in her arms.

'For my sister's new baby.' He reappeared through the doorway, his handsome features split by a wide grin. 'Silviana is my youngest sister. She gave birth to her first child—a little girl—a month ago. What's the matter?' he demanded, his voice suddenly sharp with concern. 'You're as white as a ghost.'

'I'm fine. I sat up too quickly, that's all,' she lied. 'I'm used to spending most of my time horizontal just lately,' she added, forcing a smile. 'But I don't know much about baby clothes—or babies, come to that.'

'They're not aliens from another planet,' he told her, his expression suddenly speculative as he stared at her. 'Most women would enjoy the chance to browse in a babywear shop. I know your career is important to you, Kezia, but if you're anything like my sisters you'll start to feel broody in a couple of years or so.' His tone was lightly teasing, but she stared at him levelly.

'No I won't,' she said fiercely. 'Motherhood is not for me, Nik. I can assure you of that.' She left him then, and hurried across the sitting room to her own cabin before he could see her tears.

Nik stared after her, his brows drawn into a frown. He couldn't comprehend why her words disturbed him so much, and his temper was not improved when he cut his chin on his razor, his hand strangely unsteady as he shaved.

* * *

Nik was not in their suite when Kezia returned to the ship a few hours later. He must still be talking to Captain Panos, she guessed as she took a bottle of cold water from the fridge and stepped onto the balcony. It was only a little past lunchtime, and with all the wonderful food she'd indulged in lately she was hardly hungry—not for food anyway, she amended, her cheeks growing even warmer as she recalled her hunger for the man who dominated her every waking thought.

Nik's lovemaking was becoming an addiction she would have to break some time soon. Possibly at the end of this trip. The way her heart lurched painfully in her chest at the thought was proof that she dared not allow the affair to continue. Her confidence that she could enjoy a brief fling and walk away unscathed had been sadly misplaced, she acknowledged dismally. The idea of leaving Nik tore her to shreds, but pride dictated that she should end their relationship, both as lover and employee, when they returned to England.

She could not bear to wait until he grew tired of her, always looking over her shoulder and wondering if the next attractive blonde would be her replacement in the bedroom. As his PA, would he expect her to buy her own flowers and a suitably expensive trinket? she wondered cynically. No, Nik had more respect for her than that, she reminded herself impatiently. And she couldn't blame him; he'd made it clear from the beginning that he was not in the market for long-term commitment—a sentiment she'd assured him she shared. Unfortunately her stupid heart seemed to have a will of its own and it had given itself completely and irrevocably to a man whose family were desperate for him to one day produce an heir.

It was a case of history repeating itself, she thought sadly, remembering her engagement to Charlie and the reason they had ended their relationship. She had promised herself she would never put herself in such a position again, which was why, as soon as the *Atlanta* docked at Southampton, she would tell Nik it was over.

A knock on the door dragged her from her pit of dark thoughts, and she quickly crossed the sitting room to answer it.

'Charlie! I thought you were flying home today,' she murmured distractedly to the fair-haired young Englishman standing in the doorway. Her mind was still clinging to memories of the past, but inherent good manners made her add, 'Won't you come in?'

'My flight's not until this evening, but I'm going to spend the afternoon in Rome. I didn't want to leave without saying goodbye, Kezia,' he said gently as he studied the shadows in her eyes. 'Are you okay? You look upset.' He hesitated fractionally, and then continued, 'Is it Niarchou? I couldn't help but notice that he's obviously more than your boss, but I'm afraid he's not in your league, Kez.'

'What would *you* know, Charlie? It's two years since we split up, and I've changed a lot in that time. I'm tougher than you think,' she told him sharply. 'I can handle Nik.'

'I hope so, because to me you appear the same sweet girl I knew—and I'd hate to see you get hurt.'

'For the second time, you mean?' she queried, instantly regretting her sarcasm when Charlie blushed.

'I'm sorry. I shouldn't have come here,' he muttered awkwardly. 'And, as you've so rightly pointed out, I'm the last person to give you advice on your love-life.'

He turned to go, his shoulders slumped in a way that reminded her of a small boy who'd been caught misbehaving. Charlie hadn't changed, she thought with a smile as she put her hand on his arm.

'I'm the one who should apologise. I've got a few things on my mind at the moment,' she admitted ruefully. 'I'm glad you're here, because I bought a present for your little boy.' She crossed to the table and picked up a smart little sailor suit. 'It looks a bit big, but I suppose he'll grow into it,' she said doubtfully. 'I don't spend a lot of time in baby shops.'

'Kez! I don't know what to say.' Charlie smiled warmly as he held up the suit. 'This is great—thank you. I'm sorry about…everything.' He shrugged helplessly. 'I wish things could be different for you.'

'They're not. I can't have children. But there are plenty of people a lot worse off than me.' She gave a determinedly bright smile and he slipped his arm around her shoulders.

'You're a beautiful person, Kezia—inside and

out,' Charlie told her softly. 'Take care.' His kiss was a fleeting caress to seal their friendship, but a slight noise from the doorway caught Kezia's attention, and she jerked out of his arms as she met Nik's furious gaze.

'Charlie was just saying goodbye. He's leaving today,' she explained falteringly, her temper flickering into life as Nik continued to stare at her as if she was something unpleasant swimming about at the bottom of a pond. 'I bought a present for his new baby,' she added pointedly.

'And now it must be time for you to leave, Mr Pemberton.' Nik ignored her and addressed Charlie in a tone that caused the younger man to edge hastily towards the door. 'You don't want to miss your flight.'

'You seem to be making a habit of being rude to my friends,' Kezia snapped as soon as Charlie had gone.

'Just the one friend. And on each occasion I have caught you in his arms. I think that quali-fies as an excuse for any rudeness, don't you?' he queried mildly as he crossed to the fridge and extracted a beer.

'No, I don't. I could have been rolling around

stark naked on the carpet with him and it still wouldn't have given you an excuse to speak to him like you did.' She glared at him, hands on her hips, while her hair flew around her shoulders like a halo of fire. 'You wanted a no-strings relationship—remember? You can't go and move the goal-posts when it suits you.'

The intrinsic truth of her statement did nothing to improve Nik's temper, he acknowledged grimly as violent anger coursed through him. And the fact that he was not supposed to feel jealous of Pemberton only added to his irritation.

'Have you always had such a hang-up about commitment? Or is it a result of the split with your ex-fiancé?' he growled as he stalked through to his stateroom.

'*Me* have a hang-up? That's rich, coming from a man whose most successful relationships can be counted in weeks rather than months!' Kezia followed him into his cabin, her anger melting away as she watched him unbutton his shirt. 'I've told you; Charlie's just a friend now. I admit I was upset for quite a while after our relationship ended, but I understood the reasons, and I was over him a long time ago.'

'What *were* the reasons?' Nik queried as he shrugged out of his shirt and released the button at the waistband of his trousers. 'Do you have some horrible habit that I haven't yet discovered?'

'No—!' She broke off, her cheeks scarlet. Now was an ideal time to reveal her secret, to tell him about the illness that had struck her as a teenager, and the devastating consequences of the treatment. 'I've told you already—his parents didn't approve of me,' she muttered as her nerve failed her.

She searched frantically for a way to change the subject, her eyes widening as he stepped out of his trousers. His skin had darkened to the colour of bronze, and she felt the familiar weakness flood through her as she imagined running her hands over his chest, following the path of dark hairs over his abdomen to the edge of his silk boxers.

'We can't solve every argument we have with sex,' she said breathlessly, some external force propelling her towards the bed.

'I hadn't intended to,' he replied smoothly, his eyes narrowing on the hectic colour of her cheeks. 'I was just getting changed.'

Too late she noticed the pair of khaki shorts on

the bed, and felt sick with mortification. 'Of course. My mistake,' she muttered, wishing a hole would appear in the floor and swallow her up.

He let her suffer for thirty seconds, before strolling round the bed and snaking an arm around her waist as she made to escape. 'I'm intrigued by the idea of you rolling around on the carpet stark naked. Would you care to give a demonstration?'

She bit her lip, torn between the desire to run away and hide, and the more basic urge to lay her head on his chest and absorb his masculine strength.

'I only do it on special occasions. It's hell for friction burns,' she told him gravely, and caught the answering glint of amusement in his eyes before he captured her mouth and initiated a slow, thorough exploration that left her boneless in his arms.

'It'll have to be the bed, then,' he said a shade regretfully, and he tumbled her backwards and instantly covered her body with his own, his boxers doing nothing to disguise the proof of his arousal.

This could not continue, Kezia thought faintly as she assisted in the removal of her clothes and tugged the offending boxers over his hips. She could not spend her life as a mindless sex slave, unable and unwilling to resist him. But the alternative—to live without him—would be unbearable.

There was still another week until they returned to England, and she could only pray that it would be enough time to free her heart from the silken web he had spun around it.

CHAPTER NINE

THE BAY OF NAPLES, with its sparkling blue waters and Mount Vesuvius looming in the distance, was a breathtaking sight. The city was a vibrant, colourful place, brimming with history, and renowned among other things for being the home of pizza.

Kezia found it a magical place, and was determined to do as much sightseeing as possible. But although the sunshine was glorious, the heat sapped her energy, and she was glad when Nik led the way back to the harbour.

'Do you want to go back to the ship? Or shall we have lunch here?' he asked as he tucked a stray curl beneath the brim of the straw hat he'd insisted she wear at all times. 'You look warm, *pedhaki mou.*'

'Be honest—I look like a boiled lobster,' she replied dryly.

Her face was hot, her feet ached, and she'd

managed to drip ice cream down her skirt. Nik, on the other hand, looked cool and eye-catchingly gorgeous in cream chinos and a pale blue shirt that contrasted with the golden hue of his skin. With his glossy dark hair and designer shades, he drew admiring glances from women of all ages, and Kezia was tempted to stick a sign on his forehead saying—*Hands off!* It wasn't easy for a mere mortal to partner a demi-god, she acknowledged ruefully, although to be fair Nik had been faultlessly attentive.

'We could try that little restaurant by the water's edge,' she suggested. 'It's so lovely here, and cooler than in the town.'

The sea breeze tugged at her hat and played with the hem of her skirt, lifting it to reveal a length of slim leg that was the immediate focus of Nik's attention.

'Perhaps we should return to the *Atlanta* and have a lie-down?' he murmured, the frankly sensual quality of his tone and the familiar gleam in his eyes sending a quiver of excitement through her.

'Later,' she told him firmly, fighting the urge to head back to the ship by the fastest route possible, even if it meant swimming across the harbour. She could *not* give in to her hunger for him at every opportunity, she reminded herself, ignoring the voice in her head that was counting down the days they had left before they returned to England.

'Spoilsport,' he teased as he threaded his fingers through hers and led the way across the harbour.

He was a tactile, affectionate lover, and she relished the easy familiarity of their relationship. He slowed his pace in time with hers, walking so close to her that their thighs brushed. He was so tall, the width of his shoulders so formidable, that other men kept a respectful distance, and she loved the feeling that she was utterly protected. She loved *him,* she accepted, and felt her heart miss a beat at the hopelessness of it all.

There was no future for them. To Nik, she was just one in a long line of sexual encounters, and although she believed he cared for her in his way, he would never love her. It was ridiculous to wish for the moon.

The moped speeding through the bustling harbour was no different from the dozens of others she had noticed weaving manically through the narrow streets of Naples. Kezia took scant notice of it until it screeched to a halt a few feet from her, and only then did she feel a jolt of apprehension as she stared at the two figures whose features were concealed behind their helmets.

'*Signorina!*'

She half turned, and blinked as a flashbulb momentarily blinded her.

'What...? Nik, what was all that about?' she queried faintly as the moped sped away, narrowly missing running over her toes.

'Damn paparazzi! Although they won't live long if they continue to drive like that,' he said grimly, as the pillion passenger swung round and pointed a camera at them. 'Are you all right, *pedhaki mou?*'

'I'm fine. But why were they taking pictures of us?'

Nik's face had hardened, and he seemed suddenly remote when he glanced down at her. 'The Niarchou Group's new ship has attracted a lot of attention in the press,' he said, failing to add that he, the chairman of the company, was also of considerable fascination to certain elements of the media. 'Forget it,' he urged as he noticed her obvious concern. 'They were probably taking pictures of the *Atlanta* and wanted a couple of shots of tourists on the voyage.'

'I suppose so,' Kezia murmured, but throughout lunch she could not throw off a feeling of unease.

She was certain she had noticed the distinctive pattern on the helmets of the moped rider and his companion in the town earlier that day. She was probably imagining things, she told herself impatiently. There were literally hundreds of mopeds whizzing around Naples, and the idea that she and Nik were being stalked was fanciful nonsense.

By the time they returned to the ship, to spend a leisurely evening watching a show, she had almost forgotten the incident in the harbour. Nik seemed distracted, but he made love to her that night with such skilful dedication that nothing else mattered but assuaging her desperate need for him.

He could very easily become her reason for living, she thought sleepily as the last ripples of her orgasm left her limp beneath him. When he moved to ease away from her she wrapped her arms around his neck, revelling in the weight of him. She felt him smile against her skin, and he captured her mouth in a slow, sweet kiss that drugged her senses.

'I'm too heavy for you, *agape mou.* You'll have to let me go before I hurt you.'

The truth of his last statement made her heart ache, and she kissed him with a fervour that shook them both. Murmuring something in Greek, he rolled onto his back and instantly scooped her against his chest, his lips gentle on her brow before exhaustion claimed them.

They spent the next two days at sea as the *Atlanta* journeyed to Athens. Kezia was looking forward to visiting Nik's homeland, eager to learn as much as she could about the country he was so proud of. He had promised to take her to the Acropolis, she remembered as she stirred and opened her eyes before rolling onto her side to wish him good morning.

The bed was empty, and she sat up, instantly awake. It was the first time since she had shared his room that she had woken alone, and she was shocked by her reaction. She felt as though a black cloud had covered the sun and all joy had been drained from the day because she was denied the pleasure of his first kiss.

Voices sounded from the sitting room, and she

paused to snatch up her robe before heading for the door. She could make out a torrent of voluble Greek. Nik sounded in a furious mood, and she wondered who he was yelling at down the phone. She was unprepared for the sight of him fully dressed in an impeccably tailored grey suit. With him was an older man—also Greek, she guessed—who surveyed her curiously as she stepped out of the bedroom. A tide of colour flooded her cheeks as she fumbled to fasten the belt of her robe, and her eyes were wide with confusion and growing apprehension as she stared at Nik's grim expression.

'What is it? What's wrong?' she demanded, and heard him sigh heavily as he swung away from her to stare moodily out to sea.

'You'll have to see them some time, so I suppose it may as well be now,' he said obliquely, before swinging back and thrusting a newspaper into her hands.

With a feeling of dread Kezia took it from him, her face turning ashen when she glanced at the photograph on the front page.

'My God!'

Her first thought was that she looked

enormous. The picture was a close up—so close up, in fact, that the camera lens was practically inside her bikini top—and she groaned at the sight of her breasts spilling out of the tiny triangles of material. She wasn't sure where the photo had been taken—possibly Nice, she guessed, as she stared at the shot of her and Nik frolicking in the waves. It could have been worse, she conceded, remembering another occasion when he had pulled her into the sea and untied her bikini top. At least she retained some iota of modesty in this photo.

But as she glanced at Nik's furious face her heart sank. 'What does the caption say?' she asked, recognising the Greek alphabet, but unable to read the words.

'That particular one reads—*"On the job! Niarchou boss gets personal with his assistant!"'* he translated, no glimmer of amusement in his voice. 'There are others.'

'So I see.' She sifted through the pile of newspapers on the table with shaking hands. There was some consolation that they had only made the front pages of the Greek papers, but the photo and others like it appeared inside all the British tabloids, as well as most of the other European papers. 'The men on the motorbike,' she whispered, her memory of the faceless individuals hiding beneath their helmets returning to haunt her. 'But why—?'

She broke off and swung her gaze from the photos to Nik. She knew why—he was the chairman of a multimillion-pound empire and the subject of intense interest both in Britain and abroad. Pictures of him cavorting in the surf with his secretary would have been a great scoop for the photographer, who had no doubt sold them for a small fortune.

'It's not the end of the world,' she ventured at last, when she could stand the tense silence no more. 'It's just a few pictures.'

'Several million pounds have been wiped off the company's share value since trading began this morning,' he told her coolly. 'Shareholders don't react kindly to the sight of their chairman flaunting his mistress on the company's flagship—especially when that mistress is also a representative of the company.'

'I see.' Kezia paled at the harshness of his tone. 'But what can we do now that the pictures have been published?' She knew he was angry but the idea that he somehow blamed *her* was unbearable.

'The most important thing is to initiate a damage limitation exercise. This is Christos Dimitriou, one of the Niarchou Group's top lawyers.' Nik briefly introduced her to the older man, who had so far remained silent.

Feeling acutely embarrassed, Kezia gripped the lapels of her robe together and shook hands with the unsmiling Greek.

'Christos is seeking an injunction to prevent the publication of any more photographs. Meanwhile, we'll leave the ship as soon as possible,' Nik continued, in the same clipped tone.

'I'll go and pack,' she said quickly, glad of the excuse to return to her cabin as her heart splintered. It was over, she acknowledged bleakly. Nik was a typically proud Greek and he would hate feeling a fool. The pictures of the two of them spread across every newspaper spelled the end of the brief happiness they had shared.

'The maid is already packing for you,' he informed her. 'Go and get dressed. The helicopter will be here in twenty minutes.'

'Are we flying straight back to England?' The thought of leaving the secure cocoon of the ship terrified her. For more than two weeks the *Atlanta* had provided a haven away from the rest of the world—a place where she had found her private nirvana in Nik's arms. How would she survive without him? she wondered despairingly. He was the love of her life, but she could not return to Otterbourne House as his full-time secretary and some time mistress.

Nik's jaw tightened as he noted the mixture of shame and misery in her eyes. She had no reason to feel ashamed, he brooded furiously. He was thankful she could not understand most of the scurrilous newspaper articles that suggested she was little more than a common tart, enjoying a freebie holiday and getting paid for sleeping with her boss. It was a foul insinuation, and he clenched his fists in impotent rage before quickly hiding the English paper at the bottom of the pile, until he could safely destroy it.

The whole mess was *his* fault, he acknowledged bleakly. He should have guessed that the paparazzi would be curious about the Niarchou heir's new companion. It would be impossible to protect Kezia from the press once they left the ship; he knew only too well of the lengths journalists would go to in their bid for more pictures. There was only one place he could take her until the furore died down, but he had a feeling she wasn't going to like it.

'We're not going to England,' he informed her briskly. 'My family own a private Aegean island. The helicopter will fly us to Zathos, where we'll be out of reach of the media.'

'But what about your family? Will they be there?' Kezia queried cautiously as she struggled to keep up with a situation that was fast running out of her control.

'Of course—they're looking forward to meeting you.'

'Oh, come on!' She laughed bitterly. 'How will you introduce me—secretary or strumpet? Perhaps you'll explain that I currently fill both roles in your life? Although the second is on a strictly temporary basis,' she added fiercely.

'My parents are as appalled as I am that our relationship has been vilified in the press,' he snapped. But she ignored the warning glitter in his eyes and glared at him. Pride was all she had left, and she was determined to hang on to it.

'We don't have a relationship,' she reminded him. 'You're always telling me your parents long for you to meet a nice Greek girl. You can't turn up with your PA, whom you just happen to be sleeping with at the moment.'

'If it's not a relationship, how would you describe what we share, Kezia *mou?*' he queried silkily, his anger all the more unnerving because of the tight control he imposed on it. 'If you believe it's just sex…' he paused and flicked a glance at his watch '…we may as well make the most of the fifteen minutes before the helicopter arrives and enjoy one last session.'

'Nik!' His crudeness was almost as shocking as his implication that they shared something deeper than sexual compatibility, and her confusion was tangible as she stared at him.

She couldn't be having this conversation—especially with the grim-faced Greek lawyer as a spectator she thought wildly. She didn't know how much English Mr Dimitriou understood, but she was acutely aware of his presence.

'Think very carefully about your answer,

pedhaki mou,' Nik bade her softly, his sudden movement catching her off guard as he jerked her against his chest.

'I don't know what you want from me,' she whispered, afraid to blink in case he should see her tears. 'It wasn't meant to be like this.'

When they'd first become lovers she had accepted that all he was offering was a casual fling, and had steeled herself for their inevitable parting. Incredibly, it now seemed that Nik hoped to further their relationship—but to what end? she wondered as her heart lurched in her chest. There could be no real future for them—not least because he was the last Niarchou and he needed an heir.

The sheen of tears turned her eyes the colour of aquamarine. Nik felt his gut twist as his anger drained away and was replaced with compassion. The emotional attachment he felt to her had taken him by surprise too. He understood the puzzled despair in her voice when she'd cried that it wasn't meant to be like this. At first he'd also assumed that he would be content with a brief affair, but with every passing day that he spent with her he'd found she was becoming in-

creasingly important to him. They had something special, something he'd never experienced
before, and if he was honest he wasn't sure what
he wanted to do about it.

He stared at the tremulous curve of her mouth,
glimpsed the uncertainty in her eyes, and recognised with stark clarity that he could not let her go.

'Go and get dressed,' he ordered, the sudden
tenderness in his voice causing a solitary tear to
roll down her cheek. 'We'll talk about this later.'
He caught the tear with his thumb-pad before
cupping her face in his hands, but as his head
lowered she caught sight of the stack of newspapers and gave a low moan.

The media had turned something beautiful into
a grubby scandal, and she couldn't bear for him
to kiss her. She felt sullied, her privacy exposed
in the most repugnant way, and with a strength
born of desperation she tore out of his arms and
fled to her cabin.

The helicopter flew above the brilliant blue
waters of the Aegean towards an island that
formed the only land mass as far as the eye could
see. Zathos appeared on the horizon like an

emerald set in a crystalline sea, and as they came in low over the coast Kezia held her breath and prayed they did not clip the treetops.

Her nerves fluttered as they dipped down over a hilltop, and she spied a tiny village of white flat-roofed houses that glinted in the sunshine like sugar cubes. At any other time she would have enjoyed the flight, and the wonderful views afforded by the glass bubble of the helicopter cockpit, but as they started to descend apprehension choked her.

She turned to Nik, who was sitting grim-faced beside her, and reached into her handbag. 'I think I should give you this,' she said quietly.

'What is it?' He sounded faintly bored, and made no move to take the handwritten document from her fingers.

'My resignation; I'll look for another position as soon as we get back to England.'

His eyes glinted with mocking amusement as he took the letter and ripped in two. 'If you're bored with the missionary position, I'm more than happy to spice up our love-life, *pedhaki mou*. You should have said,' he drawled sardonically.

'Damn you, Nik, I'm being serious,' she hissed

furiously. 'It's over between us, and the sooner you explain to your parents that the newspaper articles were a misunderstanding the better.'

'The hell it's over.'

He sprang before she had time to react, his hand gripping her nape as he captured her mouth in a devastating assault. She knew the futility of fighting him when his strength easily out-matched hers, and instead forced herself to remain passive. His tongue probed the mutinous line of her lips before forcing entry, and she swallowed a sob of frustration as heat flooded through her veins. Sensing her capitulation, he deepened the kiss to a level that was provoca-tively sensual until she melted against him, any idea of resistance forgotten as she responded with a desperation she could not disguise.

Only when she was utterly pliant in his arms did he ease the pressure, his tongue tracing the swollen contours of her mouth before he lifted his head. The fierce gleam in his eyes warned of his implacable determination to bend her to his will.

'Look at me and tell me this means nothing to you,' he demanded, his expression softening slightly when she stared at him in stunned silence. 'During the past few weeks you've come to mean more to me than any women I've ever met. Who knows where this might lead?' he murmured thickly, as he stroked an errant curl from her cheek.

'It won't lead anywhere. It can't,' she replied on a note of pure panic. Nik was offering her a glimpse of heaven but she was agonisingly aware of the hell that would surely follow once he knew the truth about her. He wasn't suggesting that their relationship could lead to marriage, she re-assured herself. But what if he fell in love with her? His confession that she meant something to him had shaken her to the core. This was Nik, the man with a heart of stone, who changed his women as regularly as most men changed their socks. She'd never meant for him to love her, and for one glorious second she imagined what it would be like to hear him say those words, to give her love freely and without fear of rejection in return.

Reality intruded, and she tore her gaze from the heartbreaking tenderness in his. She had been through this once with Charlie—had allowed her hopes to build, only to have them cruelly shattered when he had decided that having a family was more important to him than marrying her. She couldn't bear that level of pain again, she thought bleakly, not with Nik.

'What are you so afraid of, *agape mou?*' he queried gently. 'Do you think I'll hurt you like your fiancé once did?'

'I think it's very likely,' she replied bluntly, her voice sounding over-loud in her ears as the helicopter fell silent and she realised that they had landed.

Nik cupped her chin and stared into her eyes, as if determined to make her believe him. 'I'm not Charlie. You can trust me, Kezia *mou.* All I'm asking is for a chance to prove it.'

'I forgot to mention it's my sister's birthday,' he said ten minutes later, as the car transporting them from the helicopter landing pad swept through the gates of a huge white-walled villa. 'Everyone will be here.'

'Everyone?' Kezia queried faintly, staring in wonder at the profusion of vibrant pink flowers that covered the walls of the house. Bougainvillea, she guessed, and growing alongside it jasmine, with delicate creamy blooms and a heady fragrance that filled the air.

She followed Nik across the gravel driveway that led around the side of the house, her steps slowing as he pushed open a gate leading to an enormous, immaculately kept garden. The entire population of Zathos seemed to be assembled on the lawn, but her eyes were drawn to the gazebo and the frail looking man seated in a wheelchair in the shade. Even from a distance she noted his resemblance to Nik, and her heart thudded in her chest. She was about to meet Nik's parents, something she had never in her wildest dreams imagined would happen, and she was terrified.

What would they make of her when they must have seen the photographs of her over-exposed body in the pages of the newspapers? Did they blame her for bringing shame on Nik, and on the Niarchou name? she wondered nervously.

She wiped her damp palms on her dress, and then prayed she hadn't left a mark. The dress was of cool linen, belted at the waist, with a narrow skirt and a gently scooped neckline, and she wondered if she had subconsciously chosen white for its virginal connotations—hoping to impress Nik's parents. Some hope, she thought ruefully as she stared at the reception committee who had gathered beneath the gazebo.

'There seems to be a lot of children. They're not all your nieces and nephews, surely?' she murmured when Nik turned to her.

'I'm afraid they are. Come and meet them—they don't bite, you know,' he added gently, when she appeared rooted to the spot. He took her hand and lifted it to his mouth, his lips grazing her knuckles in a gesture that took her back to the first time she had met him at the Niarchou head office. Just as then a spark of electricity shot down her arm, and she stared at him helplessly, her heart in her eyes. 'Trust me, *pedhaki mou,* they'll love you,' he insisted, and he slid his arm around her waist and led her across the grass.

'Will they?' She could not disguise the doubt in her voice. 'Do you often bring your…' she faltered slightly '…girlfriends to meet your family?'

'I've never brought any woman to Zathos before,' he replied seriously, the velvet softness of his gaze causing her heart to perform a somersault, but as she absorbed his words they reached the group, and he tugged her forward.

'Kezia—you have a beautiful name,' Nik's father murmured in his heavily accented English, once formal introductions had been made. 'We've heard much about you—and seen quite a bit too,' he added, so softly that for a second she thought she must have misheard him.

Her startled gaze took in the glimmering amusement in his eyes, and her lips twitched. Yannis Niarchou obviously shared the same wicked sense of humour as his son, she thought wryly.

'I'm so sorry—' she began, but the old man held up his hand.

'There's no reason for you to apologise. The paparazzi are…' he shrugged his bony shoulders '…unforgivably intrusive. But my son will deal with the matter,' he said, with unwavering confidence. 'Nikos has explained everything.'

Had he? Kezia seriously doubted that Nik had explained the true nature of their relationship, and she blushed beneath his father's speculative gaze.

'You are in love with Nikos. This I see in your eyes,' Yannis explained gently as her cheeks turned scarlet. 'I am old, and stuck in this thing,' he said with a disparaging glance at his wheelchair, 'but I see plenty. I see what is in your heart, Kezia Trevellyn.'

Kezia was unable to forget Nik's father's words, and spent the rest of the day in a state of shock. Was she really so transparent? she wondered dismally. And, God forbid, was Nik also aware of her feelings for him?

Her eyes were drawn across the garden, and a dull ache formed around her heart as she watched him swing one of his little nieces onto his shoulders. The children flocked around him like bees to a honey pot, and he seemed equally fond of them, the sound of his laughter filling the air as he chased them across the lawn.

'My brother will make a wonderful father some day,' a voice murmured in her ear, and she turned to offer a tentative smile to his sister Athoula, who had joined her on the garden bench.

'He's very good with children,' Kezia replied quietly. 'I had no idea.'

'Well, he's had plenty of practice. Between us, my sisters and I have twelve little ones— although the others sensibly had theirs one at a time,' Athoula said with a grimace.

'It must have been a shock to discover you

were carrying triplets,' Kezia remarked, as she picked out the three identical little boys who were dressed in matching red shirts.

'My husband still hasn't got over it,' Athoula laughed. 'They're a handful, but I wouldn't be without them.'

Nik's sisters were nice, Kezia mused a few hours later, as she strolled down to the far end of the garden, away from the party. Indeed, every member of his family had treated her with quiet courtesy that did not fully hide their curiosity, but although they were friendly she sensed their reserve. It was to be expected, she reminded herself when she turned to watch them, her expression unconsciously wistful as she tried to imagine being part of such a close-knit family. Nik had done his best to ensure that she was included in conversation, but many of his older relatives in particular did not speak English, and in her heart she knew she was an outsider.

She suddenly longed to be back in England, where her life had been far less complicated and emotionally draining than in the weeks she'd spent with Nik. It was time to go home, but even the thought of seeing Max, the scruffy terrier she had rescued, did nothing to ease her heartache.

She watched Nik stride down the garden, her eyes focused on the chiselled beauty of his face and the inherent power of his wide shoulders. She would never love anyone the way she loved him. But for her pride's sake she had to act cool, she told herself.

'I've been looking for you,' he said a shade reproachfully as he drew her into his arms and lowered his head to initiate a slow, evocative kiss that shredded her fragile emotions. 'Stop hiding down here. Some more of my cousins have arrived and want to meet you.'

'I can't believe you have so many relatives,' she murmured when he threaded his fingers through hers and led her across the lawn.

Two little boys in red shirts suddenly ran past, from the far end of the garden, and she watched them, unaware of the shadows Nik glimpsed in her eyes, or his frown as he tried to guess the reason for her sadness.

They carried on walking towards the gazebo, but something was niggling in her mind. Two red shirts when there should have been three? she puzzled, and she glanced around the grounds of the villa in search of the third triplet.

'That gate in the far corner of the garden—where does it lead?' she asked Nik.

'To the ponds,' he replied. 'My father keeps fish, but the gate's kept locked while the children are here—for obvious reasons.'

To his astonishment he found that he was talking to thin air as Kezia tore back down the garden. She knew where she had seen the third red shirt, she remembered, a premonition of dread filling her as she reached the gate and pushed it open.

The surface of the main pond was covered with water lilies, but their beauty left her unmoved as she searched frantically for a flash of red among the reeds. She spied the infant on the opposite bank, his dark curls gleaming in the sunshine as he leaned forward to watch the fish. The second that he toppled into the water she literally flew around the edge of the pond, adrenalin coursing through her as she grabbed a handful of shirt and hauled him to safety.

'*Theos!* That was close.' Nik had followed her through the gate and was staring at her from the opposite side of the pond, admiration and another indefinable emotion in his dark gaze.

The air in the enclosed garden was curiously still, and so silent that Kezia could hear her heart pounding as reaction set in. Fortunately the child was too young to comprehend the danger he had been in, and he grinned at her happily as she lifted him into her arms and began to walk back to the gate. He was dripping wet, but she didn't care when he squirmed closer and wrapped his chubby arms around her neck. The instinct to nurture tugged at her heart, and for a second she hugged him close and rubbed her cheek on his satiny curls. Nik would one day have a son who looked just like this adorable little one, she thought, and the pain in her chest was so sharp it felt as if a knife had pierced her.

'You're an amazing woman, you know that?' he murmured softly as he lifted the child onto his shoulders and slipped his arm around her waist. 'You put on this act that you're not interested in children and then spend the entire day acting as mother hen, watching over the brood. My family have much to thank you for—and I've a feeling they're about to do so right now,' he added dryly, as the entire Niarchou clan raced across the lawn towards them.

Athoula was in tears, and there seemed to be a furious row going on between various relatives over who had unlocked the gate, but as Kezia stood, looking dazed, Nik's mother pushed to the fore and enveloped her in a suffocating embrace.

'You saved my grandson's life, Kezia, and now you will always have a place in my heart,' she announced in her broken English. 'She's a good girl, huh?' she demanded, as she turned to the rest of her family, and then, as an aside to Nik, 'She'll make a wonderful mother; she's got good hips.'

For Kezia it was the last straw, and with a cry she ran towards the villa. She had no idea where to go. All she knew was that she had to get away from Nik before her heart cracked open.

CHAPTER TEN

TODAY SHE WOULD TELL NIK she wanted to go home Kezia vowed, the minute she opened her eyes. Pale rays of sunlight filtered between the blinds as dawn heralded another glorious day on Zathos, but she couldn't stay here any longer. A week had passed since they had arrived at his parents' villa. Seven long nights spent tossing and turning in her lonely bed while he slept in his own room at the far end of the corridor.

Separate rooms was not his choice, he'd told her, his frustration evident in the fierce hunger of his kiss when he escorted her to her room each night. But his mother was old-fashioned, and out of respect for her he could not make love to Kezia under his parents' roof.

She understood his reasons, and loved him all the more for his sensitivity, she acknowledged with a sigh. But if she'd hoped that a week without the exquisite pleasure of his lovemaking would lessen his grip on her emotions she was disappointed. Since that first day, when he had followed her into the villa and demanded to know why she was crying, they had spent every waking moment in each other's company. It had been relatively easy to convince him that her tears had been a reaction to dragging his little nephew out of the pond, but impossible to prevent herself from falling ever more deeply in love with him.

Somehow, the fact that they could not fulfil their physical desire by leaping into bed at every opportunity had intensified the emotional awareness that simmered between them. Nik cared for her; she knew it from the tenderness of his smile, the way that whenever she looked at him she found his dark gaze focused on her, sending her a message that she was afraid to decipher. And with every day that passed it was becoming harder and harder to reveal that there was no future for them because she could never give him an heir.

A light tap on her bedroom door saw her scramble out of bed, her breath catching in her throat at the sight of him leaning indolently against the wall.

'Nik! What are you doing? Do you know what the time is?' she babbled, as she sought to control the familiar pain around her heart.

His sun-bleached denims were stretched taut over his hips, his black shirt open at the throat. She would never tire of looking at him, she thought as her pulse-rate accelerated. He was so indecently good-looking that she felt weak with longing, and stepped back from the door, unconsciously hoping that he would follow her into her room.

'It's a little before six,' he replied easily, as he caught her chin and tilted her face to his. 'I thought we'd watch the sunrise together.' He covered her mouth with his own in a kiss that stirred her senses, but instead of deepening it he eased back, and smiled at her undisguised disappointment.

'I'm not dressed,' she mumbled, pink-cheeked.

'I can see that, *pedhaki mou.*' His voice was dry as his eyes skimmed her, noting the silky disarray of copper curls before focusing on the firm swell of her breasts visible beneath her thin nightdress.

Did she have any idea what a temptation she

presented? he wondered, as his body reacted with its usual eagerness to the sight of her. One week without her in his bed and he was climbing the walls. Life without her sparkling, joyous presence would be no life at all, he conceded and a gentle smile tugged his lips as he glimpsed the mixture of emotions in her eyes. He would do whatever it took to persuade her they had a future together.

'Go,' he bade her, as he swung her round and tapped her smartly on the derrière. 'You've got five minutes before I come in and get you.'

'Couldn't we have watched the sunrise just as easily from the terrace?' she asked twenty minutes later, as she followed him up a steep, rocky path that seemed more suitable for goats.

'This is the best place on Zathos,' he assured her, when she finally joined him on a vast, grassy ledge that afforded an incredible view of the sea. 'That's why I'm going to build my house here.' He had spread a blanket on the ground, and grinned as she collapsed beside him, her breath coming in sharp gasps. 'You need to work out more,' he teased, rolling onto his back and drawing her down on top of him.

'Are you really going to have a house here?' she asked, desperately trying to ignore the throbbing proof of his arousal that was pushing against her belly. Liquid heat pooled between her thighs, and she wriggled—until she realised how much he was enjoying it and glared at him.

'I certainly am. The builders start laying the foundations next week. I'll show you the plans once we've had breakfast.' His hands eased beneath the hem of her tee-shirt, and he gave a growl of approval at the discovery that she wasn't wearing a bra.

'I can't see a picnic basket,' she said thickly. 'What did you bring for breakfast?'

'You,' he replied simply, before he tugged her down and claimed her mouth in a kiss that drove everything but her overwhelming need for him from her mind.

She had been starved of him for a week, and responded to his touch with a fervour that bordered on desperation as she wrenched open his shirt buttons and ran her hands over his chest. He pushed her so that she was sitting astride him, and whipped her tee-shirt over her head, his hands skimming her chest before cupping her breasts.

'Someone might come,' she whispered fearfully, torn between her desire and the need for propriety.

'There's nobody here. Only the goats,' he told her, watching the way her eyes became glazed when he stroked his thumb-pads across her nipples until they tightened to hard peaks that begged provocatively for him to repeat the action with his tongue. He drew her forward and captured one distended peak between his lips, loving the way she ground her hips against him when he suckled her.

'You don't know how desperately I've longed to do this,' he muttered, his voice muffled against her throat. 'It's been the longest week of my life, *agape mou,* and if I don't have you right now I think I'll explode.'

'Don't explode just yet,' she urged, as she obligingly wiggled her hips so that he could tug her shorts down her legs. With a muffled oath he flipped her onto her back, shrugged out of his jeans and boxers and dispensed with her briefs with a deftness that left her trembling and exposed to his gaze.

'You are so very lovely, Kezia *mou.*'

He trailed his hand over her stomach and

gently eased her legs apart, so that he could dip between them, his fingers parting her with delicate precision to discover her moist inner heat. Kezia half closed her eyes and gave herself up to pure sensation as he explored her with a thoroughness that drove her to the brink. She could smell the sweetness of the grass mingled with the faint tang of the sea, the air cool and clear as the sun streaked the sky with streaks of pink. There was something elemental, almost pagan about lying naked beneath the heavens, and as Nik moved over her she stared at him, her emotions stripped bare.

'I want you, Nik,' she whispered, and he needed no second bidding as he nudged her thighs apart and entered her with one powerful thrust.

Instantly her muscles closed around him, drawing him deeper as she matched his rhythm with an eagerness that had him gritting his teeth and fighting to hang on to his control. Their bodies moved with total accord in a primal dance as old as man. Above them the sky lost its first rosy blush as the sun rose and filtered through the leaves of the olive trees, dappling their entwined limbs with gentle warmth.

Kezia clung to Nik's shoulders as he increased his pace and drove into her, faster, deeper, until her breath burst from her body in painful gasps, her whole being focused on reaching that magical place she had only experienced with him. Suddenly she arched beneath him, trembling on the brink of ecstasy, and as she tumbled over he caught her cries with his mouth, his tongue mimicking the fierce thrusts of his body with a degree of eroticism that stunned her.

Wave after wave of pleasure engulfed her, but still he kept his steady rhythm, so that he took her up once more, her second orgasm so intense that it seemed almost impossible to withstand. Only then, when she sobbed his name over and over, did his control splinter, with spectacular results, and a feral groan was ripped from his throat to be carried away on the breeze.

Her first conscious thought as she drifted back down to reality was that she had given herself away this time. She had made love to him with her heart as well as her body, and as she held him close and listened to his ragged breathing gradually return to normal, she was filled with tenderness. The moments after a man had experienced sexual release were said to be his most vulnerable, and she crossed her hands over his back in a gesture of protection. She would willingly give her life for him, she acknowledged, as the tears that had gathered behind her eyelids overspilled.

He caught them with the finger he trailed down her cheek, his eyes darkening with emotion.

'Will you marry me?'

Her shock was so great that she could have sworn the earth actually tilted on its axis. She wondered if she had misheard him, wondered if he was making some sort of cruel joke, but the intentness of his expression warned her he was deadly serious.

'Why?' she croaked, sounding as though she had swallowed glass.

His smile stole the breath from her body, and for a few seconds she allowed herself to believe the impossible—that fairytales did exist and there could be a happy ending for them.

'Because I love you, *pedhaki mou,*' he murmured, his lips grazing her collarbone before trailing a path to her earlobe. 'Sometimes I think I've loved you for ever, but for a long time I fought it,' he admitted ruefully. 'From the day I first met you, valiantly trying to make excuses for your alcoholic boss, I was hooked.'

He rolled onto his side and scooped her up against his chest, his fingers threading through her hair as if he could not bear to be apart from her.

'At first I assumed it was simply physical,' he continued with frank honesty. 'I couldn't wait to get my hands on your lush body, and I told myself I would be content with a brief affair. But you crept under my guard, Kezia. I found that I wanted to be with you every minute of the day, as well as the night, and the passion we shared was only part of the joy I felt in your company. Why are you crying?' he asked softly as the tears slid unchecked down her face. 'I want you to be my wife, to live here with me in the house that we'll build…'

'To be the mother of your children?' Kezia finished for him, and she tore out of his arms and forced her stiff limbs into her clothes.

'At some point in the future I would hope we would consider starting a family,' he said, his voice cooler now, his expression no longer gentle, but tinged with suspicion and a degree of hurt that shredded her emotions. 'But not straight away, *agape mou*—I know how much you value your independence, and there's no reason why you shouldn't continue with your career for a few more years.'

'Nik, I can't,' she burst out, needing to say the words now, before her will-power deserted her. She pulled on her shoes and stood, staring down at his naked form. He looked like a Greek god, his skin gleaming like bronze, and already she could feel herself weakening.

'You can't what?' he demanded harshly, reaching for his clothes.

She had assumed he would start to dress, but instead he pulled a small velvet box from the pocket of his jeans and held it out to her.

'Before you say any more, this is for you. It's proof, if you need it, that I'm serious. I want to marry you, Kezia, despite the fact that you seem to view the idea as a fate worse than death,' he added sardonically.

With shaking fingers she flicked open the box to reveal a brilliant sapphire surrounded by diamonds that reflected the fire of the sun. Its beauty pierced her soul, and she bit back a sob of utter despair. 'I can't marry you,' she whispered as she snapped the box shut and thrust it at him. 'I'm sorry.'

He jumped to his feet then, and dragged his jeans over his hips before rounding on her. 'Why the hell not?' he growled savagely. '*Theos,* Kezia, I've spent most of my adult life determined to avoid matrimony. The irony of your rejection isn't lost on me,' he added darkly. 'It's Pemberton, isn't it?' he muttered, a nerve working in his cheek. 'You've never got over the fact that he married another woman. Are you still in love with him? Is that it? Or did he hurt you so badly that you're afraid to give your trust again?' His expression softened as he moved towards her, his hand outstretched, as if he was approaching a particularly nervous colt. 'I swear I'll never hurt you, *pedhaki mou.* I love you, and I know you feel something for me too. You just have to find the courage to look into your heart.'

Her heart was about to splinter into a thousand pieces, Kezia thought wildly as she jerked away from him and began to scramble down the steep path. He was right behind her, and she knew that if he caught her in his arms she would be lost. For his sake she had to deny her feelings for him.

'You're wrong, Nik,' she cried over her shoulder, slipping and sliding down the dusty path. 'I don't love you and I never will. I don't want to marry you—do you hear?'

His blistering reply burned a hole in her heart that she knew would never heal, but a desperate glance revealed he had given up the chase and had stopped dead on the brow of the hill, as if he had been hewn from marble.

Later, Kezia could recollect little of her wild flight back to the villa, of throwing a few basic essentials into her case and changing into loose cotton trousers and a shirt that were comfortable to travel in.

In the sanctuary of her room a little of her sanity returned, bringing with it the temptation to tell Nik the real reason she had turned down his proposal. He had told her he loved her—not just with words but with his body, she realized, as she remembered the way he had made love to her with such reverence that her eyes had filled with tears. In return she had cruelly rejected him by denying that she loved him.

Surely she owed him the truth about her feelings for him? All she needed was courage, he'd told her. But where he was concerned she had none. She could not bear to see his face when she revealed that she would never be able to give him a child. Shock would turn to dismay, followed by undisguised relief that she had refused to become his wife. Even worse, he might feel a mixture of guilt and pity that she would find unbearable. He had nothing to feel guilty about. He'd made no secret of the fact that he was under considerable pressure to produce the next Niarchou heir, and her infertility was a problem that would eventually destroy their relationship.

In a torment of indecision she finally poured out the reason she had turned him down in a letter, giving details of the illness she had suffered as a teenager and the devastating consequences of her treatment. She kept it brief and unemotional, hoping that he would simply accept that there was no future for them and move on with his life. She did not reveal that hers would be empty and utterly joyless without him.

For once the villa was quiet. Nik's parents had travelled to Athens, so that Yannis could attend the hospital, and they planned to stay overnight in the capital. Of Nik there was no sign. None of the staff had seen him that morning, one of the maids explained, unable to disguise her surprise when Kezia asked how she could get to the mainland. The boatman, Stavros took some persuading and only agreed to ferry her across the water when she assured him that Nik knew she was leaving.

As the boat chugged across the waves she turned and stared at Zathos until it disappeared from view, her eyes burning with tears that she finally let fall.

Otterbourne House basked in the early summer sunshine, its sandstone walls glowing mellow and warmly inviting. Kezia parked her Mini on the driveway and glanced up at the graceful pillars that stood on either side of the front door. She had fallen in love with the house with almost the same intensity with which she'd lost her heart to its owner, and the knowledge that this was her last visit tore at her already fragile emotions. At least she had Max, she consoled herself, her spirits lifting slightly at the thought of seeing the scruffy little terrier again.

She had arrived back at her flat the previous afternoon, after a nightmare journey from Greece, during which she had been forced to spend twelve hours at Athens airport, waiting for a cancellation. By the time she'd reached home she'd been mentally and physically drained, and had worked her way through a box of tissues as she poured out her heart to her sympathetic flatmate, Anna. And now she faced the pressing problem of searching for a new flat as well as another job. Anna had decided to move to the US for six months, to fulfil several lucrative modelling contracts.

There was no real reason for her to stay in the London area, Kezia brooded. She loved the countryside, although the exclusive area of Hertfordshire where Otterbourne was situated was out of her price bracket. And for the sake of her sanity she needed to live as far away from Nik as possible—Scotland seemed tempting, and maybe she would find a place with a garden for Max.

'I'm sure he sensed you were coming.' Nik's housekeeper, Mrs Jessop laughed when she opened the front door, and Max shot down the steps, barking excitedly as he leapt into Kezia's arms. 'He's been restless since you phoned this morning.'

'Oh, Max—did you miss me?' Kezia murmured as she hugged his wiry little body. 'I'll never leave you again, I promise.' The dog wagged its tail and bounded back into the hall, pausing in the doorway as if waiting for her to follow him.

'Why don't you wait in the study while I go and get his basket and lead?' Mrs Jessop invited.

It was a perfectly reasonable request, and Kezia forced herself to walk up the front steps, unable to explain her reluctance to enter the house that held so many memories of Nik.

'Would you like a cup of tea?'

'No, I have to leave as soon as possible. I'm flat-hunting,' she said apologetically as she pushed open the door of the study.

Max ran off after the housekeeper, leaving her alone in the sun-filled room that Nik had chosen as his office. Coming here had not been a good idea, she acknowledged as she fumbled in her bag for the letter she'd written to him and placed it on the desk. If she closed her eyes she could almost imagine he was here, his dark gaze glinting with the mixture of amusement and simmering sexual awareness she remembered so well, his voice deep and sensual to her ears.

'You seem to be making a habit of leaving letters for me.' The familiar drawl sounded from behind her and she whirled round, her eyes huge and shocked in her white face. 'Perhaps you should consider a career in the postal service?' Nik added sardonically, his expression unfathomable as he surveyed her.

'What are you doing here?' she whispered, sounding so indignant that his fury lessened a degree.

'I live here,' he reminded her laconically. 'I flew back on my private jet the minute I'd read the note you left for me on Zathos. Why are *you* here?' he demanded harshly.

'I came to deliver my resignation letter. You tore up the last one,' she reminded him huskily, unable to tear her eyes from him. In black tailored trousers and matching silk shirt he was so breathtaking that the pain in her chest intensified.

'I won't make the same mistake again,' he assured her coolly, and he strolled over to his desk and picked up the letter. 'In the circumstances, I think we can dispense with the formality of a month's notice, don't you? You're free to go whenever you like, *pedhaki mou*.'

The careless endearment, coupled with the faintly bored expression on his face, tore her apart. She had expected anger, but his indifference made her want to weep. So much for his declaration that he loved her, she thought bleakly. He certainly didn't appear to be heartbroken that they would never see one another again. But of course now he knew the secret she had kept from him throughout their relationship, he was no doubt relieved to be shot of her.

'I'll just collect Max and I'll be off,' she mumbled, dragging her eyes from him to stare at the carpet while she blinked back her tears.

Nik studied the dejected slump of her shoulders and fought the urge to drag her into his arms. She was fiercely proud, and would reject him out of hand if she thought he pitied her. Right now he was torn between the desire to shake some sense into her stubborn, obstinate body and kissing her senseless, but neither action would guarantee him the prize he was utterly determined to win.

'You can't take Max, I'm afraid,' he told her briskly. 'He's my dog and he belongs at Otterbourne.'

'But...you don't even like dogs,' Kezia said shakily. 'You once said Max looks like a floor mop, and he *isn't* yours—I found him.'

'And *I* paid a ridiculous price for him to that rogue farmer who realised I'd give him whatever he demanded.'

'You did that...for me?' A warm feeling crept around her heart at the realisation that even back then he must have cared for her. 'Then let me take him, Nik?' she pleaded. 'I love Max.'

'Lucky Max,' Nik snapped, his patience close to breaking point. 'There's only one way you can have him. If you marry me you can lay claim to all my worldly goods—including my dog.'

The flare of emotion in his eyes was too much, and she wrapped her arms around her body, as if she could somehow prevent herself from falling apart. 'You know why I can't,' she whispered. 'You're the last Niarchou; your family are depending on you to provide an heir.

'To hell with my family,' he swore savagely. 'They're important to me, yes,' he continued, when she stared at him in stunned silence, 'but not as important as the way I feel about you,

Kezia *mou*. Between them my sisters have provided my parents with a dozen grandchildren. There's a whole future generation who will grow up and one day help run the company.'

'But I saw the way you were with your nieces and nephews, Nik,' she said brokenly. 'You love children, and nothing will convince me that you hadn't hoped to have a family of your own one day.'

'I won't lie to you,' he said gently, moving closer, so that she found herself backed up against his desk with nowhere to run. 'I'd blithely assumed that the gift of children would be granted to me in the same way that I've been blessed with so much else in my life. But a child isn't a foregone right. I didn't fall in love with you because I viewed you as a brood mare. I love you for your bravery and honesty, for the fact that you are utterly loyal and so generous that I feel humbled when I'm with you.' His voice cracked with emotion, his face working as he laid his heart bare, but it was the tremor of his hand as he gently smoothed her hair from her face that brought fresh tears to Kezia's eyes. 'You ended your engagement when your fiancé learned that you couldn't have children, didn't you?' he murmured softly.

She nodded. 'I wanted to tell you, but at first it didn't seem necessary. I assumed we would have a brief fling—sex without the complication of emotional involvement—but I was lost from the start,' she admitted sadly. 'I love you so much it scares me,' she whispered, one solitary tear sliding down her cheek. 'That's why I won't marry you, Nik. My infertility isn't something that can be cured, and I won't allow you to sacrifice your chance to have a family just because you feel sorry for me— What are you doing?' she cried fearfully, when he suddenly swung her into his arms and strode towards the door.

'I'd wondered if that was the reason you'd turned down my proposal,' he said, his tender smile taking her breath away. 'Or rather, I hoped,' he added huskily, as he relived the agony of her rejection and the pain he'd felt for her when he had read her letter.

It had taken less than a minute for him to accept that her inability to have children made no difference to his love for her. If anything he loved her more, he acknowledged silently as he glimpsed the uncertainty in her eyes, the vulnerability that made him ache with the need to protect and care for her for the rest of his life.

'You are my life, *pedhaki mou*,' he told her as he took the stairs at a steady pace and headed with implacable determination for his bedroom. 'You are the only woman I will ever marry, so you'd better get used to the idea.'

He dropped a tantalisingly brief kiss on her lips, shouldered the door and dropped her unceremoniously in the centre of the bed, his body instantly covering hers before she could escape. This time his kiss lasted longer, so sweetly evocative that her defences crumbled and she clung to him, unable to stem her tears.

'Who knows what the future holds?' he whispered as he trailed his lips over her damp cheeks. 'All I care is that we share it, side by side, the joys and the disappointments. We may even be blessed with a family.' He laid a finger against her lips as she shook her head. 'There are thousands of children in the world who need parents to love them.'

'You mean we could adopt?' The little flame of hope inside her blazed into life, and her smile was filled with the emotions she could no longer deny. 'I love you so much, Nik.'

Simple words that meant the world to him, he acknowledged, and he closed his eyes briefly and felt an unfamiliar stinging sensation behind his eyelids. He shrugged out of his clothes and dispensed with hers with hands that shook slightly, his body instantly hardening as he studied her voluptuous curves. His woman—for eternity, he vowed, as he reached for the small box on the bedside table, opened it, and took out the sapphire that glowed with the intense blue of the Aegean.

'Nik, are you sure?' Kezia whispered, the shadows not quite banished from her eyes as she stared down at the ring he had slipped onto her finger.

'I've never been more sure of anything in my life.'

The fierce intensity of his response dealt with the last of her fears, and she inhaled sharply as he trailed a sensuous path from her mouth to her breasts. They swelled in his hands, aching for his possession, and as he anointed one tight bud and then the other with his lips she rubbed her hips urgently against his and pleaded for him to make love to her.

'Nik!' She groaned her frustration when he moved over her, but held back from pushing the hard length of his arousal deep inside her.

'Not yet, *agape mou,*' he muttered hoarsely. 'Not until you've said the words I need to hear.'

'I love you,' she cried, moved to tears by the edge of uncertainty in his voice.

'And you'll marry me?' His control was slipping, and sweat beaded his brow as he stared down at her, his love for her blazing in his dark eyes.

'Yes.' She sighed her pleasure as he entered her, slow and deep, filling her. 'But only if you promise never to stop doing that.'

'You have my word, *agape mou,*' he vowed, and then there was nothing but sensation, soft murmurs of pleasure that built inexorably to a crescendo, and finally the whispered pledges of everlasting love.

EPILOGUE

'NIKOS ALWAYS SAID he'd build a house here.' Yannis laughed as he stared out over the sweeping gardens of the recently completed villa on Zathos to the sparkling sea beyond. 'Even as a small boy he knew what he wanted, and he was determined to get it.'

Kezia smiled at her father-in-law as she tucked a blanket around his knees. 'Are you warm enough?' she fussed, aware that the old man had grown frailer in the past year. 'The sun's not very hot this early in the spring.'

'He wanted you for his wife. I saw it in his eyes the first time he brought you here,' Yannis confided, his expression filled with genuine affection as he glanced at her, and then across the garden to his son.

Kezia followed his gaze, and felt the familiar

softening of her heart as Nik strolled across the lawn. The child in his arms was eighteen months old, with the same glossy black hair and dark eyes as his father. The resemblance between them was uncanny, she thought, as she smiled at her son, but perhaps not entirely unexpected, when most Greek men shared similar characteristics.

The adoption agency had no details about little Theo's biological parents. He had been found, wrapped in a shawl, in the entrance of a hospital on the mainland, and her heart ached for the woman who had been driven by unknown circumstances to abandon her baby. Theo had spent the first nine months of his life with foster parents, but the moment she had cradled him in her arms Kezia had been overwhelmed with love for him. With the documentation finally complete, Theo was now officially a member of the Niarchou family, and she was looking forward to taking him to Otterbourne to meet Max, later in the summer.

'He's utterly fearless on that swing, you know,' Nik said proudly as he handed her their son and leaned down to kiss her with barely concealed desire. 'With any luck he'll have a nap this afternoon—like his grandfather,' he added when Yannis emitted a snore.

'We'll have an hour to ourselves,' Kezia murmured lightly. 'What would you like to do?'

'I'll give you three guesses,' he replied, the gleam in his eyes sending a quiver of excitement through her as she rocked her son to sleep.

Life couldn't get any more joyous than this, she thought dreamily. But a short while later Nik proved that it could!

MILLS & BOON® PUBLISH EIGHT LARGE PRINT TITLES A MONTH. THESE ARE THE EIGHT TITLES FOR MAY 2007

———— ❧ ————

THE ITALIAN'S FUTURE BRIDE
Michelle Reid

PLEASURED IN THE BILLIONAIRE'S BED
Miranda Lee

BLACKMAILED BY DIAMONDS, BOUND BY MARRIAGE
Sarah Morgan

THE GREEK BOSS'S BRIDE
Chantelle Shaw

OUTBACK MAN SEEKS WIFE
Margaret Way

THE NANNY AND THE SHEIKH
Barbara McMahon

THE BUSINESSMAN'S BRIDE
Jackie Braun

MEANT-TO-BE MOTHER
Ally Blake

MILLS & BOON®

0407 Rom LP

MILLS & BOON® PUBLISH EIGHT LARGE PRINT TITLES A MONTH. THESE ARE THE EIGHT TITLES FOR JUNE 2007.

TAKEN BY THE SHEIKH
Penny Jordan

THE GREEK'S VIRGIN
Trish Morey

THE FORCED BRIDE
Sara Craven

BEDDED AND WEDDED FOR REVENGE
Melanie Milburne

RANCHER AND PROTECTOR
Judy Christenberry

THE VALENTINE BRIDE
Liz Fielding

ONE SUMMER IN ITALY...
Lucy Gordon

CROWNED: AN ORDINARY GIRL
Natasha Oakley

MILLS & BOON®

0507 Rom LP